JANE WITHERS AND THE HIDDEN ROOM

Jane Withers

and

The Hidden Room

An original story featuring
JANE WITHERS
famous motion-picture star
as the heroine

By ELEANOR PACKER

Illustrated by HENRY E. VALLELY

Authorized Edition

WHITMAN PUBLISHING COMPANY
RACINE, WISCONSIN

CONTENTS

ILLUSTRATIONS

A Slim Girl Stepped to the Platform

JANE WITHERS
and The Hidden Room

CHAPTER ONE

SOMETHING STRANGE

The little village of Hollytown-on-the-Hudson dozed in the Indian summer warmth of the late October sunshine.

It was four o'clock and the small railroad station at the edge of the village was almost deserted in the mid-afternoon lull. Only one car was waiting in the graveled parking space, a shiny station wagon with the words "HOLLY HALL" in small letters on its door. Only two people stood on the long platform: one was a girl in a moss-green sweater, her hair the rich gold of honey and her brown eyes eager; the other was a youngish woman in a gray print dress and a tailored felt hat.

"Only two more minutes and she'll be here!" the girl exclaimed with a quick glance at the watch on her wrist. "I can hardly wait to see her. I wonder if she's changed much this summer."

"I don't imagine she's changed very much." The woman smiled. "It's only been three and a half months since Jane left, you know."

"It seems like a century." The girl sighed with the ex-

13

travagance of sixteen years. "Here comes the train now, Miss Brand!"

Three minutes later the train slid to a stop beside the gray stone station. One passenger, a slim girl with dark brown hair and pansy-blue eyes, stepped down to the platform.

A yellow-haired tornado in a green sweater raced toward the new arrival and hugged her with strong, young arms.

"Hi, Jane!"

"Ellin!" Jane Withers cried and the two girls smiled at each other with warm affection.

"Miss Brand's here, too," Ellin remembered after a moment.

Jane turned to shake hands with Millicent Brand, who said smilingly, "I'm glad to see you, Jane. Did you have a pleasant trip from California?"

"Wonderful!" Jane answered.

"Are you feeling completely strong and well again?" Miss Brand asked anxiously.

"Yes, thank you. To tell the truth, I never felt better in my whole life," Jane replied gaily.

"You sure are lucky, coming back a month later than the rest of us," Ellin told her with an impish little grin.

"I'm sorry I had to be so late, Miss Brand." As she spoke, Jane turned serious eyes toward the older woman. "But the old flu germs don't pay any attention to school schedules."

"Of course, they don't. And you'll easily make up the classes you've missed," Miss Brand assured her. "All the teachers will be glad to help you."

"Jane's missed more than studies." Ellin twinkled while saying this.

"What?" Jane asked quickly.

"There's a big surprise waiting for you at dear old Holly Hall, Miss Withers," Ellin told her with mock solemnity.

Jane pivoted questioningly from Ellin to Miss Brand. "What is it?" she asked.

"I'm sure I don't know what Ellin means." Miss Brand shook her head, but a faint, rosy flush was spreading slowly across her cheeks.

"P. B.," Ellin hissed mysteriously.

"Oh." The flush deepened from Miss Brand's rounded chin to the edge of her chestnut hair. At that moment she didn't look like a dignified professor of English Literature at the exclusive school for "young ladies," Holly Hall.

"What's P. B.?" Jane demanded. "You simply have to tell me, Ellin. What *is* it?"

"You'll find out," Ellin answered airily. "Come on, Janie. Henry is waiting for your bags."

Jane turned to greet the smiling colored man in the neat, gray uniform.

Henry beamed, picking up Jane's luggage and leading the way to the station wagon. "Welcome home, Miss

Jane."

Jane followed Miss Brand into the car and Ellin perched on the seat in front of them.

"We have the same old room, Jane," Ellin said, turning to face the other two. "I've brought a lot of stuff to fix it up. I hope you'll like it."

Jane smiled as the station wagon rolled along the main street of Hollytown-on-the-Hudson. "I know I will."

It was a pleasant small town, nestled in a curve of the Hudson River, and it managed to blend the picturesque quaintness of its past with the up-to-date briskness of its present. The smartly modern shops along its one main street were housed in century-old buildings of stone and brick and weathered timber. Long, sleek cars were parked in front of ancient hitching posts.

Hollytown's greatest pride was Holly Hall, the "school for young ladies," which had been founded by Miss Abigail Ramsdell the First, seventy-odd years before in the old stone Ramsdell house, built on a tree-shaded knoll two miles north of the village. The school had soon outgrown the house and, one by one, three new buildings had been built on the knoll. Now, weathered by fifty years and covered with ivy, the "new" buildings looked as old and mellow as the original Ramsdell homestead, which housed the unmarried members of the school's faculty.

Miss Abigail the First, had been dead for forty years, but Miss Abigail the Second, her niece and namesake, had taken her place as head mistress of Holly Hall. Grandmothers, who knew Miss Abigail the First, and whose granddaughters were being trained by Miss Abigail the Second, often shook their heads sadly and wondered to whom they could entrust the education of their great-granddaughters, since there was no Miss Abigail the Third, to carry on Holly Hall's leadership.

"Tell me about the surprise, Ellin," Jane insisted, when the station wagon had left the village and was following the wide road toward Holly Hall. "What is this mysterious P. B.?"

"P. B. is not a what. He's a man: Paul Berthon, the new professor of Romance Languages," Ellin explained, her brown eyes shining with excitement. "There's never been anything like him in the history of Holly Hall."

"Oh, I thought it was something really thrilling." Jane's voice was dull with disappointment.

"Just wait till you see him!" Ellin cried. "He's Charles Boyer, Clark Gable, Gary Cooper and Bob Taylor, all rolled into one man. Isn't he, Miss Brand?"

The professor of English Literature hesitated. "Well—." She smiled. "I don't know about that, Ellin. But he is very attractive. And he is a very brilliant man."

"I still can't understand how Abigail ever happened to take him into the school," Ellin said and giggled.

"Ellin!" Millicent Brand suddenly remembered that she was a teacher. "You must not speak disrespectfully of Miss Ramsdell. She wasn't thinking of Mr. Berthon's looks when she engaged him. He came to her with very high scholastic recommendations. Mr. Berthon may look romantic, but I understand that he is an excellent teacher and a strict disciplinarian in his classroom."

"When he looks at you, you don't care whether he's a disciplinarian, or not!" Ellin sighed with mock rapture. "At last, romance with a capital R has entered Holly Hall, Janie. And he's young, that's the best part of it."

"Mr. Berthon is not so young," Miss Brand said quickly. "He must be almost forty."

"If he were fifty, he'd still be practically an infant at Holly Hall," Ellin said with a chuckle. "With the exception of you and Miss Mercer and Mr. Berthon, there isn't anyone under sixty-five at the faculty table, Miss Brand. You know that."

"Let's discuss some other subject," Miss Brand said with a quiet firmness which silenced even Ellin. "Tell us about your trip, Jane."

The station wagon turned in between the stone pillars, which marked the entrance to Holly Hall, and rolled smoothly up the curving driveway. Jane sighed with pleasure when she saw the ivy-covered buildings of the school, standing among the trees on the knoll. She loved every inch of Holly Hall's wide, shaded lawns, sloping down to the Hudson, and every nook and corner of its paneled rooms and broad corridors.

Classes were over for the day, so, when Henry parked the car before the entrance doors, it was immediately surrounded by dozens of laughing girls.

"I'll carry youah luggage up to youah room, Miss Jane," Henry said and disappeared under a load of bags and hat boxes.

The next half hour was a haze of laughter and greetings, of questions and answers, as the girls swarmed around Jane. Then, finally, Jane was ushered into Miss Abigail Ramsdell's office with its thin, old rugs and carved, polished furniture.

The Head Mistress of Holly Hall was a frail woman with delicate features and keen, gray eyes under carefully waved white hair. She greeted Jane with a cordial smile and, as always, the girl was filled with an awed respect for the brilliant, austere woman who had guided the destinies of Holly Hall for forty years.

At last all the greetings were over and Jane was alone with Ellin in their room. It was a large, airy corner room on the third floor of the main school building and, through its diamond-paned casement windows, the girls could see the distant Hudson.

"Everything seems just the same—even Miss Abigail hasn't changed one bit," Jane sighed happily as she opened her bags. "I can't believe that we're really Juniors this year, Ellin."

Jane smiled affectionately at the girl who had been her best friend since the first day of their first year at Holly Hall, when they had arrived, bewildered and uncertain freshmen, Jane Withers from California and Ellin Dwyer from New York.

"Well, we are and we're lucky, because Mr. Berthon is teaching only junior and senior classes."

Ellin was curled in the middle of her twin bed, idly watching Jane.

"For Pete's sake, can't you forget your precious Mr. Berthon for ten minutes, Ellin Dwyer?" Jane asked, darting in and out of the closet with dresses and sweaters and coats.

"*You* won't forget him, either, after you see him," Ellin predicted merrily. "He's out of this world, Janie. You know, dark and sort of mysterious. I wonder where he came from and what sort of a life he lived before he landed at Holly Hall."

Jane laughed. "You don't mean to tell me that you haven't found out his life history yet, after being here a whole month."

"I don't think anyone knows much about him." Ellin shook her blonde head. "I asked Miss Brand. All she knows is that he was teaching in some exclusive school in England before the war. Our Abigail seems to think that it is a bright feather in her cap that she was able to grab him for Holly Hall. And you should see all the dear old ladies of our faculty, smirking and preening when he's around. Even Milly Brand goes a little ga-ga."

"Maybe we ought to get busy and promote a little romance there," Jane suggested brightly. "I hate to think of good old Milly, ending her days as an old maid school teacher, like Dr. Cornelia Stratton, for instance."

"Milly's too old for him," Ellin declared briefly.

For a long minute Jane stared at her best friend. Then she laughed gaily.

"The light begins to dawn," she cried. "But you'd better get any romantic notions out of your head, Ellin. Your mother'll swoop down and drag you out of here by your hair, not to mention what Abigail'll do."

Ellin stared dreamily into the green leaves beyond the open windows.

"You know, Jane," she said after a moment, "there's something strange about Mr. Berthon."

Jane paused in her unpacking.

"What do you mean?"

"I don't know. I can't explain it. But you'll see."

Then the dressing gong sounded and there was no more time for talking.

CHAPTER TWO

SOMETHING WRONG

When the dinner gong sounded, Jane and Ellin joined the procession of girls, trailing down the wide stairways into the dining hall. As they walked through the doors, their laughing voices were stilled and they moved with a quiet dignity into the room.

The dining hall was long and wide, with French doors opening upon a terrace. Its walls were paneled in rich, dark wood and the carpeted floor was dotted with small tables, each seating four girls. At one end of the room was the faculty table, with Miss Abigail's chair in the center, facing her "young ladies."

"I asked for permission to save a place for you at my table," Ellin whispered, leading the way to a table where two other juniors, Bunny Walters and Mary Lou Gibson, were waiting.

Soon the room was filled with girls, standing behind their chairs, awaiting the arrival of Miss Abigail.

"There he is!" Bunny Walters suddenly whispered.

As she spoke, a kind of electric excitement seemed to fill the room.

Jane looked up and saw a tall, dark man, walking with a lithe, easy stride toward the faculty table. As he took his place, facing the girls, Jane could see the lean, strong line of his cheek and jaw.

"He certainly is good-looking," Jane admitted in a whisper to Ellin.

Then, suddenly, he glanced across the room and his dark eyes met Jane's. For a moment they stared at each other. In that brief moment, a strange chill of something like fear crept over Jane. With a little shiver she remembered Ellin's unexplained words.

"There's something strange about Mr. Berthon."

Jane thought she understood what Ellin meant.

Then Mr. Berthon smiled, casually and impersonally. It was as if he had lifted a cold, hard mask from his face and revealed his friendly, handsome real self. With that smile, the chill disappeared, but Jane still trembled a little.

A moment later Miss Abigail entered the room. She was dressed in black, as always, but her face was an unnatural white in color. As she took her place at the faculty table, Jane noticed that she was biting her pale lips.

Something was wrong. Miss Abigail looked ill.

Then Miss Abigail sank into her chair and, with a rustle of low voices, the girls sat down.

"Isn't he everything I said he was?" Ellin whispered to Jane.

"Yes." Jane nodded, dragging her eyes away from Miss Abigail's tense, black-clad figure to the face of the man, sitting next to her.

He was more, far more than Ellin had prophesied, she

thought. In that one short meeting with his eyes, Jane had felt the impact of a compelling force which frightened her. Yet she knew that he had not really seen her. His eyes had looked beyond her, beyond the walls of the room —and in that look there was something so cold, so almost savage that Jane shuddered again, remembering.

During dinner Jane laughed and talked and listened to the chatter of the other three girls. Now and then she glanced toward the faculty table. Everyone looked normal, except Miss Abigail and Millicent Brand. Miss Abigail was still parchment pale and looked so ill that Jane was worried. Miss Brand was talking with a vivacity and bright-eyed eagerness which were new to her and which made her almost beautiful.

When the dinner was ended, Miss Abigail arose. But, instead of leaving the room with her usual brisk dignity, she hesitated a moment, leaning heavily on the back of her chair. Then she turned quickly, as if she had made a sudden decision, and faced the waiting girls.

"Young ladies," she said in an oddly strained voice, "an unfortunate incident took place this afternoon. I have decided that it is best to speak directly to you about it, rather than to try to maintain a secrecy which will result in unpleasant and disturbing rumors."

She paused and one slim white hand moved toward the neckline of her dress. With a start of surprise, Jane suddenly realized that the exquisite, old-fashioned diamond pin, which Miss Abigail always wore in the evenings as

"A Robbery Has Taken Place in Holly Hall."

her only ornament, was missing from the black lace dress.

"For the first time in the history of the school there has been a robbery at Holly Hall," Miss Abigail went on in her clipped, precise manner. "Sometime, late this afternoon, someone entered my room and took a small case containing several pieces of jewelry. Among them were the diamond pin with which you all are familiar, and its matching earrings. The pin and the earrings have more than a monetary value to me. They belonged to the first Miss Abigail, and to her mother and grandmother before her. I hope that I shall recover them."

Miss Abigail's voice stopped and there was a hushed, horrified silence in the dining hall. A robbery at Holly Hall! It was unbelievable.

Then Miss Abigail was speaking again:

"We have made a careful search of my rooms, hoping that, by chance, I might have misplaced them. But I am sure that the pieces of jewelry were in the case when I went to my office this morning. Understand, young ladies, I suspect no one. And no one will be questioned. If anyone of you knows anything, which might help us recover the jewelry, I shall appreciate your coming to me privately. Your confidence will be respected. Also I shall ask you to discuss the matter no more than necessary. Now, if you will pardon me—"

Miss Abigail stepped away from the table and no one moved until she had left the room. Then, with subdued voices and sober faces, the faculty members and the students walked slowly from the dining hall and gathered in small groups in the halls and on the terrace.

Jane was standing with Ellin and several other girls, talking in low shocked voices about the robbery, when Miss Brand beckoned to her.

"Since you have just arrived, I want you to meet the new member of our faculty, Jane," she said and Jane could feel the suppressed excitement in her voice.

An hour before Jane would have been excited, too, at the thought of meeting and talking to Paul Berthon. But now Miss Abigail's words had driven all other thoughts from her mind.

Then she was standing in front of Mr. Berthon, shaking his hand and listening to his deep voice, with its faint touch of a foreign accent. His eyes were smiling and friendly. That strange coldness had disappeared. Jane felt a warm liking for him and forgot completely that moment of chilled fear which she had felt in the dining hall.

Mr. Berthon spoke easily, expressing his sympathy for Miss Abigail in the loss of her family treasures.

"Of course, the fact that they are family heirlooms is of greatest importance to Miss Abigail," Miss Brand said quietly. "But they were also very valuable. All Miss Abigail's diamonds were perfect stones and she had several beautiful emeralds."

Then Miss Brand and Mr. Berthon turned the conversation into other channels and they were talking about

California when Dr. Cornelia Stratton of the Psychology Department joined them. Dr. Stratton was a forceful and determined woman and she fairly dragged Mr. Berthon away to the library to look at some book, which they had been discussing at dinner. As he bowed and left, Jane could see the sag of disappointment in Miss Brand's trim body under the blue crepe dress.

"Isn't it terrible about the robbery?" Jane whispered.

"Yes. Terrible," Miss Brand agreed, dragging her eyes back from the retreating Mr. Berthon. "But we must not discuss it, Jane. Miss Ramsdell doesn't want the school to be upset by it."

Miss Brand left to join a group of anxious-eyed teachers and Jane went back to the girls. Miss Abigail's announcement had stifled the gaiety and laughter and music which usually filled the hour between dinner and the study gong.

Gradually, by ones and twos and threes, the girls drifted away to their rooms. Soon the terrace and the halls were empty.

Slowly Jane and Ellin climbed the stairs to their room. As they rounded the curve on the second floor, the door of Miss Abigail's sitting room opened and two men, accompanied by Mrs. Gray, the housekeeper, stepped out into the hall.

"Detectives, I'll bet," Ellin whispered.

"Who do you suppose did it?" Jane asked, when they were alone in their own room with the door closed.

"Any one of a hundred people," Ellin replied, her brown eyes sober. "We'll probably never know. Especially if it turns out to be one of the girls."

"It couldn't be one of our own girls!" Jane exclaimed.

"I hope not. But you never can tell," Ellin replied thoughtfully. "And there's just a chance, too, that Miss Abigail might have mislaid them and that they'll turn up in some unexpected place."

"Not Miss Abigail. She never mislays anything." Jane shook her brown head emphatically and bent to pick up a hat box which she had left near the door.

Suddenly she dropped the box, clutched Ellin's arm and uttered a choked cry.

"Look!" she gasped, pointing.

A small glittering object lay on the beige rug just inside the door.

"It's one of Miss Abigail's diamond earrings!" Jane whispered.

CHAPTER THREE

P. B.

Jane and Ellin stood in Miss Abigail's sitting room and looked down at the crumpled figure of Holly Hall's Head Mistress huddled in a chair beside the fireplace. Miss Abigail seemed to have shrunk and grown old in the last few hours. Her slim, erect figure was stooped and her keen eyes were dimmed.

"Think carefully, girls," she said, glancing from the gleaming earring, which she held in her hand, to the two worried, young faces. "Are you sure that you can't remember any possible way in which the earring might have been taken into your room?"

"We've thought and thought, and we can't even imagine a way, Miss Abigail," Jane said slowly. "We don't even have any idea when it was put there. It might have been done while we were at dinner, or later. It might even have been put there before we went up to the room. You see, the place was sort of cluttered with my bags and boxes and things. It was under the hat box, so we couldn't have seen it."

"Did you move the hat box when you were unpacking before dinner?"

"I don't think so," Jane replied, after a moment's thought. "I didn't have time to do much unpacking."

"Who carried the bags and boxes up to your room?" There was sudden eagerness in Miss Abigail's voice.

"Henry, I think. Yes, I'm sure he did. The truck men carried up the trunk, but Henry took up the lighter bags and the two hat boxes."

"Yes, of course." Miss Abigail's tones were dull and lifeless again. Then she added, as if talking to herself, "Henry has been with us for fifteen years. I don't think he could know anything about it."

"Of course not," Ellen said with firm loyalty. "It was probably put there by the real thief."

"I suppose you mean that someone was deliberately trying to point suspicion toward you two girls," Miss Abigail spoke slowly.

"Yes, that's what Ellin means, but maybe it wasn't done deliberately, at all, Miss Abigail," Jane suggested quickly. "Maybe the earring just happened to get caught in the cord around the box and then dropped off, when I lifted the box."

"Yes," Ellin added excitedly. "Maybe the thief dropped it in his hurry and, as Jane says, it just happened to get caught in the cord."

"That's a possibility." Miss Abigail nodded thoughtfully. "But it must have happened between the station and your room. Can you girls remember all the places where the hat box was?"

"I think I can," Jane answered. "The porter set it down on the platform with my other luggage. Henry carried it to the station wagon. Then, so far as I know, he carried it directly from the station wagon up the stairs to the room. Of course, he might have set it down somewhere in the halls or on the stairs."

"I shall report all these possibilities to the investigators for the insurance company," Miss Abigail said quietly.

"Oh, Miss Ramsdell, I do wish that you would have the investigators or the police or someone search our room," Ellin cried. "We've looked everywhere, but we can't find anything else."

"I'm sure that, if there were anything else, you girls would have found it," Miss Abigail said firmly. "No one is going to search your room, or any room. I have complete confidence in you and in all the young ladies. And I believe that, eventually, the missing case will be found, so I am determined that the school shall not be disturbed by forced searches. Now, please go back to your studies, girls, and try, if possible, to forget what has happened. If I need your help, I shall call on you. And I appreciate your coming to me so promptly."

Jane and Ellin murmured, "Yes, Miss Ramsdell. Good night," and turned toward the door.

"Girls!" Miss Abigail's voice stopped them. "I wish that you would not tell anyone of the finding of the earring. I shall appreciate your saying nothing until we can make a thorough investigation."

"We won't say a word, Miss Ramsdell," the girls promised.

"Miss Abigail's a wonderful woman, but she sure is old-fashioned," Ellin whispered as the two girls walked slowly up the stairs to their room. "If I'd lost all that valuable stuff, I'd turn the school upside down until I found it. She may have absolute confidence in her dear young ladies, but there are two or three girls here that I wouldn't hold above suspicion."

"That's exactly the reason Miss Abigail doesn't want us to talk about the robbery, Ellin," Jane said sensibly. "She knows that, if we talk about it among ourselves, there are sure to be whispers and suspicions. I honestly think Miss Abigail would rather lose those precious heirlooms forever, than have one of her innocent girls suspected."

"Maybe you're right, Janie," Ellin agreed with a sigh. "But most people aren't as noble and high-minded as Miss Abigail. And you know as well as I do that they're going to *think* suspicions, even if they don't *say* them."

Back in their room, the girls made a half-hearted attempt to study, but it was impossible.

"Let's look around again," Ellin suggested finally. "Maybe we missed something that might be a clue."

So, for the second time, they painstakingly searched every square inch of their room and the furniture and Jane's luggage. But they found nothing.

Finally, the "lights-out" gong sounded in the hall. The girls switched off the lamps, undressed and slid into their twin beds. They talked in low murmurs for awhile. Then gradually, Ellin's voice died away into a drowsy whisper.

"Mr. Berthon!" Jane Whispered to Herself

Long after Ellin was asleep Jane lay wide awake in the darkness. When the luminous hands of her bedside clock pointed to midnight, she crept out of bed and walked to the window. The moon was shining, making sharply etched shadows on the lawn. Jane stared out into the black and silver peace of the night and tried to remember everything that had happened since she stepped off the train that afternoon, hoping to find some clue to the earring's strange appearance in the room.

Suddenly her eyes centered on a deep shadow under an oak tree, far down the curve of the driveway. The shadow was moving and, as Jane watched, it separated into two splotches of darkness. One black shape walked rapidly and silently between the trees toward the Faculty Cottage. The other slipped in the opposite direction toward the garages and stables.

Jane's eyes followed the first figure. There was something familiar about the lithe, quick stride.

"Mr. Berthon!" Jane whispered to herself in startled surprise.

The second figure suddenly stepped into a bright patch of moonlight and Jane saw the unmistakable gray of a chauffeur's uniform. Then the shape dissolved in the black shadows of the shrubbery.

"*Henry* and Mr. Berthon!" Jane murmured with amazed bewilderment.

She strained her eyes in a quick survey of the lawn, but there was no other movement in the quiet night.

At last, with a little sigh, she went back to bed and, finally, fell asleep.

The next morning she told Ellin what she had seen. Ellin listened, her brown eyes wide with interest and excitement.

"What do you think it meant, Mr. Berthon and Henry meeting like that in the middle of the night?" Ellin cried in a low voice.

"I don't know," Jane answered. "It might mean a lot and it might mean nothing."

"What are you going to do about it?" Ellin asked eagerly. "Are you going to tell Miss Abigail?"

"Not yet," Jane replied in a low voice. "I thought and thought about it before I went to sleep. And I decided that the best thing to do was to say nothing until I'd had a chance to talk to Henry and, maybe, to Mr. Berthon."

"Are you going to ask them about it?" Ellin whispered.

"Not in so many words," Jane told her. "I'll do it in a roundabout way without their knowing that I've seen anything. Maybe I can find out more that way than by direct questions. Besides, if there's anything mysterious about their meeting, they wouldn't tell the truth, probably, if I did ask them."

"That's true." Ellen bit her soft lips thoughtfully. "Is there anything I can do?"

"Nothing, except keep quiet. Promise me, Ellin, that you won't say a word to anyone, not even to Bunny and

Mary Lou, until I tell you what I've found out."

"I promise, Jane," Ellin said solemnly.

Ellin kept her promise, even though at the breakfast table and between classes the girls talked of nothing except the loss of Miss Abigail's jewelry.

In the fifteen-minute interval between the last morning class and luncheon Jane slipped out to the garage. Henry, covered with a heavy blue overall, was busily washing one of the faculty cars.

"Good mahnin', Miss Jane," he said with a wide grin. "Anything I can do foh you this mahnin'?"

"Do you mind if I look in the station wagon, Henry?" Jane asked. "I've lost a—a glove and I thought I might have dropped it yesterday, coming from the station."

"It wasn't theah, I'm suah," Henry told her. "I already breshed out the station wagon an' washed it. I didn' see no glove. Mebbe you left it on the train, Miss Jane."

"I probably did," Jane agreed. "I was so excited, getting back to school, that it's a wonder I didn't leave more than a glove. It's a new station wagon, isn't it, Henry?"

"Yes'm. Miss Ramsdell bought it jest this last summah. It's biggah than the old one. I carry a whole passel of you girls to the movies now on Satuhday aftahnoons."

"Does anyone drive the station wagon except you, Henry?"

"Sometimes. One of the teachahs. Mostly the youngah ones, like Miss Brand. But usually I drives it. Keeps me pretty busy too, hauling folks back and fohth to the station in Hollytown. Yestiday I made three trips. The last time I took in a bunch of magazine writin' folks that had come out heah to look at the architectoor of the school. They went back to New Yawk jes befoah you come."

"Does Mr. Berthon ever use the station wagon?" Jane asked after a moment's pause.

"Not hahdly evah. He's got his own cah. That theah l'il coop." Henry pointed to a small car in the corner of the garage. "He's a funny fella, that Mr. Berthon," he added with a rich chuckle. "Always takin' long walks at night or kitin' around the country in that l'il ole coop."

"Do you like to take walks, too, Henry?" Jane asked with elaborate casualness.

"No'm, not me!" Henry laughed and shook his graying head. "I'm gettin' too old foh walkin', Miss Jane."

"What do you do at nights, Henry?" Jane asked with smiling interest. "Surely you don't stay around the school every night in the week."

"Most nights I do." Henry's brown eyes looked into Jane's with honest directness. "Once in a while I go into the village, but that's usually on an errand foh Miss Ramsdell or some of the teachahs. An' then I allays drives the cah. No walkin' foh me. An' I'm allays home by 'leven. Miss Ramsdell don' like the help out late, 'cept when we get special pehmission."

"So Miss Ramsdell's strict with you, too, is she?" Jane smiled.

"She's strict. But she's the grandest lady that evah lived." There was such honest sincerity in Henry's tones that Jane was ashamed of her suspicions and her questions.

"She is wonderful, Henry. You're right," Jane said warmly. "Do you mind if I take one little peek in the station wagon, Henry? Maybe there's just a chance you might have overlooked that glove and it's one of my best ones."

"Go right ahead and peek all you want, Miss Jane. But I'm suah that I'd seen it, if it had been theah."

Jane hurried over to the station wagon. She pretended to inspect the entire floor, but she looked most carefully at the space between the rear seats, where Henry had placed her bags and hat boxes. Henry had done a good job of sweeping. There wasn't a trace of anything, even dust, in the station wagon.

As Jane turned away from the car, the luncheon gong sounded.

"You're right, Henry. It isn't there. If you see anything of the glove, a dark blue kid one, please let me know, will you? Thanks."

Then Jane ran toward the school building. Ellin was waiting for her at the entrance to the dining hall.

"Where have you been?" she asked quickly.

"Talking to Henry," Jane whispered.

"Did you find out anything?"

Jane shook her head.

"I'll tell you all about it later," she promised quickly, as Bunny and Mary Lou joined them.

Jane was so silent at the luncheon table that Bunny finally said, "What's the matter with you, Janie? Don't you feel well?"

"I have a little headache," Jane replied. "I guess I'm just tired after the long trip and all the excitement of last night. I'll be all right tomorrow."

The other three girls returned to their low-voiced discussion of their various ideas about the finding of the thief who had taken Miss Ramsdell's case, and Jane looked toward the faculty table. Miss Ramsdell was in her usual place, but she looked even paler and more ill than she had the night before. Mr. Berthon was sitting beside her and Jane could see the grave sympathy in his handsome face as he spoke to the frail, white-haired woman.

Jane knew, looking at Mr. Berthon and remembering Henry's honest face, that she must have been mistaken. It couldn't have been Mr. Berthon and Henry meeting in stealthy silence in the midnight quiet. If it had been, there was doubtlessly some good reason for their meeting. It could have had no possible connection with the theft of Miss Abigail's precious jewelry. She'd better forget about it and look somewhere else for a clue, if she was going to play school detective.

But how had that earring found its way under the hat box in her room?

"Did you girls see those magazine writers who were here yesterday?" Jane asked the others, suddenly remembering what Henry had said about driving them to the station.

Bunny and Mary Lou noddod.

Ellin answered, "Yes, there were two of them. They drove to the station with Miss Brand and me, when we went to meet you, Jane. Their train left just before yours arrived. Why?"

"Oh, nothing in particular." Jane shrugged her shoulders. "I heard someone say that some writers had been here."

"They were doing a story about the architecture and decorations of Holly Hall for a magazine," Ellin explained. "All the way to the station they raved about the lines and symmetry and all that stuff. They must have been somebody important, because Miss Abigail herself received them."

"They were two old fluffs, if you ask me," Bunny volunteered. "I saw them, coming out of Miss Abigail's apartment. Then they made a tour of some of the girls' rooms."

"Evidently they didn't think much of the girls' rooms," Ellin laughed. "You should have heard their remarks about the atrocious taste of modern youth in the decorative arts. The man wasn't so bad. But the woman chattered on and on, until I thought even good old Milly would explode. I hate would-be highbrows, don't you?"

Miss Ramsdell arose and left the room. The girls followed.

"Now for the best hour of the day," Mary Lou giggled as the four walked across the lawn. "Romance, Languages, three B."

For a moment the thought of Paul Berthon drove the robbery from their minds and the girls were smiling when they entered his classroom.

Mr. Berthon was sitting at his desk and Jane walked toward him.

"My name is Withers, Jane Withers," she said in her clear voice. "I am reporting to the class a month late because of illness."

"Yes, of course, Miss Jane," Mr. Berthon smiled. "Miss Ramsdell explained the matter to me. So did your very good friend, Miss Brand. I am happy to have you with us and I shall be glad to do anything I can to help you in making up the work which you have missed."

"Thank you, Mr. Berthon," Jane said and found a vacant seat.

She sat, fascinated, during the hour of that class. There was no doubt that Paul Berthon was the most attractive man whom she had ever seen. Several times their eyes met and he smiled. But, she noticed, he smiled just as pleasantly and casually at all the other girls. She wished with all her young heart that she were older and startlingly beautiful, so that he would notice her especially.

"Gosh! That's the only short hour in the whole day!" Bunny Walters sighed as the girls trooped from the class-

"My Name Is Jane Withers," She Told Mr. Berthon

room.

"And now comes psychology with dear, dear Dr. Stratton," Mary Lou reminded them and they all shuddered.

The psychology class was dismissed at last and Jane and Ellin sauntered slowly across the lawn through the October sunshine. It was the last class of the day and they had a half hour of free time before they were scheduled to report on the tennis courts.

"Now tell me what you found out from Henry, before we run into any of the other girls," Ellin demanded eagerly.

Briefly Jane repeated all that Henry had said.

"I know now that I was silly, even to think that good old Henry might have been wandering around on some suspicious midnight business. As for Mr. Berthon, he was probably just taking one of his regular night walks."

"And he probably met one of the gardeners, or someone, coming back late and trying to slip across the lawn without being seen," Ellin added. "But why were you so interested in those magazine writers, Jane? I could tell that there was something on your mind, when you asked those questions this noon."

"I just wondered about them, that's all," Jane replied, her face serious. "They were strangers. They were in Miss Abigail's room. They rode in the station wagon. My hat box was in the station wagon."

"Well, if you are trying to make some kind of a connection between those two old mossbacks and the diamond earring, you're on the wrong trail," Ellin said emphatically. "If you had seen them, Janie, you'd realize that they didn't have enough sense to steal candy from a baby, much less diamonds from Miss Abigail. They may know all about architectural lines and symmetry, but that's all they do know. They were the most self-satisfied, smuggest pair I've even seen."

"We don't seem to be getting anywhere, do we?" Jane sighed dismally. She glanced up and added, "Here comes Henry in the station wagon now. I wonder where he's going."

The girls stepped quickly across the driveway as the station wagon rolled past.

In the seat behind Henry sat Mr. Berthon. He was leaning forward, talking so earnestly to Henry that he did not notice Jane and Ellin, standing beside the driveway and looking at him with staringly wide eyes.

CHAPTER FOUR

A TALK IN THE DARK

Dinner that night was an unusually silent meal. Miss Abigail did not appear. Dr. Cornelia Stratton presided in her place.

"Miss Ramsdell wished me to say that she is very sorry that she will not be able to be with us this evening," Dr. Stratton announced briefly.

As they sat down, Jane and Ellin looked at each other, a silent question in their eyes.

Even the presence of Paul Berthon at the faculty table could not relieve the hushed gloom which filled the pleasant room. To the girls Miss Abigail *was* Holly Hall and, without her, nothing seemed right or normal.

After dinner the girls wandered aimlessly around the halls and terraces. The October night was warm and the twilight was long and peaceful.

Jane was sitting on a low balustrade, when she suddenly saw Paul Berthon walking quickly across the lawns toward the river.

"I'll be back in a minute, girls," she said quickly to Ellin and the others. "I have some pictures up in the room that I want to show you."

Jane hurried into the hall. But she didn't go upstairs to her room. Instead, she walked quickly across the deserted dining room, slipped through the open French windows and out onto the lawn on the other side of the building. Then she ran toward the path along the river bank, concealing herself as much as possible behind the shrubbery and trees so that the girls on the terrace would not see her.

When she reached the wide path, which followed the curve of the river, she slackened her pace and sauntered slowly, as if she were enjoying a leisurely evening stroll. This was the direction in which Mr. Berthon had walked. Soon she must catch a glimpse of him.

Suddenly, in the twilight stillness, Jane heard the murmur of low voices. She quickened her pace. She rounded a curve in the path and saw Mr. Berthon, sitting on a stone bench, looking out across the river. But he was alone.

"I must have been imagining voices," Jane whispered to herself and slowed her steps again to an idle stroll.

Mr. Berthon looked up as Jane drew nearer to him.

"Good evening," he said, rising. "Are you taking an after-dinner walk, too?"

"Yes," Jane replied with a bright smile. "It is so beautiful at this time of the evening, just before real night comes."

"It is my favorite time of day, the twilight," Mr. Berthon said. "Will you share my bench, Miss Jane?"

As Jane sat down, there was a muffled crackling of dry branches on the slope below them.

"What's that?" she asked, startled.

It sounded as if someone were moving rapidly away down to the river. Jane remembered the voices which she had thought she had heard.

"Probably some little animal, hurrying homeward in the dark," Mr. Berthon said easily and sat beside her.

His smile was so friendly and open that Jane was sure that the crackling of the underbrush *must* have been caused by some animal. She must quiet down. She was letting her imagination and her nerves run away with her.

"I didn't know young American girls liked solitary walks and meditation," Mr. Berthon said. "I thought that they preferred gaiety and fun and good-fellowship."

"Most girls do, I guess," Jane answered, her lovely young face serious in the purple-gray dusk. "But sometimes I get tired of listening to silly chatter. Besides, if I sit here and look west, I am looking toward home, you know—California."

"Don't tell me that you're homesick, too," Mr. Berthon smiled gently.

"*Too?*" Jane repeated. "Are you homesick, Mr. Berthon?"

"Yes, of course," he answered with a boyish frankness. "But not for places and things, or even for people. I'm homesick for the past, for the world as it used to be, for the world which is gone forever."

For a moment Jane was silent, impressed by the deep

sadness in his low, mellow voice.

"I suppose you do find this country a lot different than your own native land," she said finally.

"This is my native land," he replied, facing her. "I was born here in this country. My mother was an American. But I have spent a great part of my life in Europe. My father's business was there. Then the war came and changed everything and I have—"

His voice drifted into silence.

"Have come home," Jane prompted shyly.

"That's right, little Jane," he said quietly. "I have come home. It is good to feel that way."

Jane experienced a warm inner glow. He had spoken to her as if she were a person, an adult, not a mere schoolgirl to be brushed aside as unimportant because she was so young.

"Haven't you any family here?" she asked after a brief and strangely comforting silence.

"Yes. One sister, Lucienne. She lives in New York."

"Is she a teacher, too?"

"She was, in Europe. But now she is an assistant manager in a beauty shop. She has traveled a long way from textbooks to massages."

Now there was bitterness in his voice.

"I think I understand," Jane said gravely and felt very old and very wise, picturing this sister, who was probably as beautiful as Mr. Berthon was handsome, catering to the whims of selfish, beauty-mad women, while she longed for her real home and her real work.

"Do you see your sister often?" she asked.

"As often as possible. Almost every week-end. You see, we have found a little cottage, a quaint, small stone house, about a mile and a half from here on the shore road. Fortunately for us, the owner was willing to lease it for a year. So we have a place where we can be alone on the week-ends and work in our garden. It is wonderful for Lucienne, after her long week in the city."

"But I thought that you lived in Faculty Cottage," Jane said, surprised.

"I do, during the week. But I spend Saturdays and Sundays at the cottage. It is really a sort of secret, that cottage. Only a few of my fellow faculty members know about it. We are selfish, Lucienne and I. We like to have our days of leisure to ourselves, or with the few friends whom we really enjoy. I think that you can understand that, little Jane."

"Oh, I can," Jane said eagerly. "I can imagine what a relief it must be to you to get away from all us giggling schoolgirls and from the faculty, too."

She laughed softly, thinking of Dr. Cornelia Stratton.

"Not all the schoolgirls," Mr. Berthon smiled. "Some Sunday I should like to have you and your friend, Ellin, come for tea. You might bring Miss Brand along, too. I know Lucienne would enjoy meeting you."

"Oh, that would be wonderful," Jane cried enthusiastically. "Ellin and Miss Brand would love to come. And so would I."

"Ellin is your very best friend, isn't she?" Mr. Berthon asked quietly.

"Yes. She's the grandest girl I ever knew."

"Her mother seemed very nice, too. I had the pleasure of meeting her at the reception for the faculty and the parents the first week of school. The Dwyers have a home near here, haven't they?"

"Yes. It's a beautiful place, about fifteen or twenty miles north of the school. Ellin often takes me home for weekends. Her mother and dad are wonderful."

"Perhaps we shall be there together some week-end," Mr. Berthon said cheerfully. "Mrs. Dwyer was kind enough to invite me to spend some Saturday and Sunday at their home."

"When are you going?" Jane asked quickly, her eyes shining.

"Mrs. Dwyer didn't mention any definite date. So perhaps she will forget about so casual an invitation. But I am hoping that she won't. I should like to spend a day or two with a real American family in a real home, like theirs."

"Mrs. Dwyer won't forget. She never does. You'll be hearing from her soon. I'm sure you will, Mr. Berthon."

"I wish that Lucienne could have the same opportunity," Mr. Berthon sighed. "It has been so long since she has been in a home."

"I'll speak to Ellin." Jane's voice was eager. "I know

"When Are You Going?" Jane Asked Quickly

that she and her mother would be delighted to have your sister as their guest, Mr. Berthon."

"Please don't think I'm imposing, Jane." He spoke quietly. "Perhaps it would be better for you to say nothing. But my heart aches for Lucienne. At least, I have the companionship of people who speak my language. But poor Lucienne is in an alien world and she is so very lonely."

"You are lonely, too, aren't you?" Jane's voice was low and filled with sympathy.

"Yes." There was a simple directness in his deep voice and in his eyes as he looked at Jane.

"Is that why you take long walks alone?"

"Not such long walks, but alone," he answered, smiling.

"Do you ever walk late at night, when the whole world is asleep?" Jane asked, priding herself that she was keeping her words lightly casual.

"Occasionally. But why do you ask?"

Mr. Berthon's mouth was still smiling, but there was no laughter now in his dark eyes.

Jane's heart pounded. Now she would learn the truth about those moving shadows in the midnight darkness of the lawn.

"I thought I saw you last night. I couldn't sleep and I was looking out the window," Jane spoke as calmly as she could.

Mr. Berthon hesitated for the merest fraction of a

minute.

"You *did* see me," he said quietly. "I couldn't sleep, either. So, instead of looking out the window, I went outside and wandered around for awhile."

"All alone?" Jane waited for his answer, holding her breath in her anxiety.

"Of course!" he laughed. "I think all my colleagues were sleeping the deep sleep of the righteous."

Jane choked and tears burned in her eyes. She knew that Mr. Berthon was lying. Because she knew that, if he *had* been that one dark splotch in the moonlight, he had met *someone else* in the shadows under the trees.

"Why do you look at me that way, Jane?" he asked sharply, leaning forward so that his dark eyes could search her face in the deepening dusk.

"Maybe I'm just imagining things, but I thought I saw someone with you last night," she stammered, winking back the tears.

Then Mr. Berthon laughed and lightly patted her hand.

"You did. But that's a secret that I hadn't wanted to tell, because it isn't mine. But I know that it will be safe with you. It was Henry whom you saw with me. I happened to meet him as he was hurrying across the lawn to the garage. From what he said, I think that he had been out on some romantic mission and was late returning. He was very anxious that no one should find out about it. I promised him that I would keep his little secret. So you must promise, too. Why, you're trembling, Jane! Are you cold?"

"Yes, a little."

Jane's voice quivered. She was glad, and so relieved, to know that the meeting under the trees could be so easily and simply explained. She could understand why Henry had fibbed. Naturally, he didn't want to confide his personal affairs to one of the schoolgirls.

"I'm a little nervous, too," she added quickly. "All the girls are upset and jittery about the robbery."

"We all are. The faculty, too. But worrying won't bring back Miss Ramsdell's heirlooms, and besides, everything possible is being done to recover them." He stood up and smiled down at her. "Now I think you'd better go back to the school, Jane. It is almost time for the study gong. Also, I don't think that Miss Ramsdell would approve of a teacher and a student sitting in the dark on the river bank."

"No, I'm sure she wouldn't." Jane laughed without a trace of embarrassment. "But I've enjoyed our little talk, Mr. Berthon. Sometime I'd like to hear about that world which is gone forever now. Will you tell me about it?"

"Perhaps. Someday. Now, good-night, Jane."

Jane hummed happily as she ran up the path and across the lawn. She could picture Ellin's eyes, when she told her that the deep, dark mystery of the night before had turned out to be only the chance meeting of a sleepless professor and a colored chauffeur returning from an evening's visit with his lady-love, who was probably a maid in one of the big houses along the road to Holly-town-on-the-Hudson.

When Jane stepped from the dark shadows of the lawn, she saw a long car, standing on the driveway in front of the terrace steps. Then Ellin's voice called to her.

"Jane Withers! Where have you been? We've been looking everywhere for you. Mother's here and she wanted to say hello to you before she left."

Jane hurried forward to greet Ellin's mother. Mrs. Dwyer might have been her daughter's elder sister, with the same deep gold hair and dancing brown eyes.

"I stopped at the school first, to see you and Ellin, Jane, and, second, to ask permission from Miss Ramsdell for you girls to spend next week-end with us," Mrs. Dwyer explained, when the greetings were ended.

"Wonderful!" Jane cried happily.

"And what do you think, Janie?" Ellin interrupted exuberantly. "Mother's inviting Miss Brand and Mr. Berthon, too. Won't that be just too, too exciting? Mother met Mr. Berthon at the faculty reception and he promised to come out to the house any time he was invited."

"This Mr. Berthon seems to have made quite an impression on all you girls," Mrs. Dwyer smiled.

"He has," Jane admitted gaily. She hesitated a moment, then added, "I am wondering, Mrs. Dwyer, if one more week-end guest would be inconvenient?"

"Of course not, Jane. Is there someone you would like

to invite?"

"Mr. Berthon's sister."

"Why, I didn't know he even had a sister!" Ellin exclaimed in surprise.

"He told me about her this evening," Jane explained. "I went for a little walk around the grounds and I happened to meet Mr. Berthon. We talked for a few minutes. I said something about being homesick and he admitted that he was, too. Then he told me about his sister. Her name's Lucienne. She used to be a teacher, too, but now she's working in a beauty shop in New York. She's assistant manager. He said that she was very lonely. So I thought that, maybe, you might like to invite her, too."

"Of course we will," Mrs. Dwyer said cordially. "I'm writing Mr. Berthon a note tonight and I'll include his sister in the invitation. It was sweet of you to think of it, Jane."

"I feel sorry for both of them," Jane said seriously. "It must be terribly hard to be so far away from your real home."

"We'll try to make them forget their homesickness for two days, at least." Mrs. Dwyer patted Jane's hand as it rested on the car door. "Now, girls, please try not to worry too much about the loss of Miss Ramsdell's jewelry. It is a terrible thing, but there is really nothing any of you can do. I feel sure that whoever is guilty will be found, sooner or later."

The study gong sounded at that moment and Mrs.

Dwyer said good-bye.

"I certainly have a lot to tell you, Ellin," Jane whispered as the two girls hurried across the terrace and into the
hall.

When they were alone in their room, with the door
tightly closed, Jane told Ellin about her talk with Mr.
Berthon.

"And to think that we sort of suspected good old honest
Henry!" Jane sighed, when she had finished the story.

"We didn't suspect him, really," Ellin said thoughtfully.

"No, I guess we didn't, not really," Jane agreed.

Yet that night Henry disappeared, taking all his be-
longings with him and leaving a brief note addressed to
Miss Ramsdell, telling her that he was going away for
good and that he would not return.

CHAPTER FIVE

A VERY SILENT GUEST

The Georgian house of the Dwyers, with its rosy brick walls and white shutters, stood on a tree-shaded knoll overlooking the Hudson River. Terraces and gardens sloped down to the water. At one side of the house there was a crescent-shaped swimming pool, its clear water shimmering with the blue-green tint of its tiles.

The Dwyers and their week-end guests gathered beside the pool in the sunshine of Saturday afternoon. The Indian summer warmth was still in the air. Jane and Ellin splashed merrily in the water while their elders lounged in low, cushioned chairs.

Ellin's father, his stocky, active body dressed in tennis flannels, sat beside Paul Berthon and talked of war conditions in America and Europe. Mr. Berthon leaned back comfortably in his chair, his deep-set eyes glowing under the thin, black line of his brows.

The three women sat a few feet away from the men, interrupting their own conversation to call occasionally to the girls in the pool. Margaret Dwyer and Millicent Brand wore tennis dresses. Lucienne Berthon was wearing beautifully tailored white slacks, with a scarlet ribbon around her black hair. She talked very little, but her slow smile took the place of friendliness engendered by conversation. She lay back indolently in a deep basket chair and watched the others under lowered, long-lashed eyelids.

Except for her black hair and her long, slender body, Lucienne was utterly unlike her brother. Her eyes were a cold gray-green, instead of his warm brown. Her movements were slow and studied, entirely different from his quick litheness.

She had arrived, looking very smart in tailored blue, just before luncheon. The others, Miss Brand, Mr. Berthon and the girls, had driven up that morning from the school in the car, which Mrs. Dwyer had sent for them, and they had waited on the terrace for Lucienne. She had said almost nothing, had smiled a great deal and, by the time luncheon was served, had seemed as much at home as if she had spent every week-end at the Dwyer house.

After luncheon she had changed from her traveling clothes into slacks and had joined the others at the tennis courts, where she had watched the games and listened to the conversation with that same smiling, agreeable silence.

"I wonder what Lucienne's thinking," Jane whispered to Ellin, as they pulled themselves out of the water on the opposite side of the pool and sat on the warm tiles.

"She's the silentest person I've ever seen," Ellin said and smiled.

"But she doesn't miss a trick with those funny eyes of hers," Jane remarked in a low voice. "When I went

Lucienne Lay Back and Watched the Others

into the house for a handkerchief, while we were playing tennis, I saw her wandering through the rooms. She was coming out after changing her clothes. But she was stopping on the way to look at everything. 'Lovely place, isn't it?' she said to me and wandered on outdoors. I'll bet she could draw a blueprint of the house, if she had to do it. She's nice and pleasant and all that, but there's something about her I don't quite like, Ellin."

"You're not jealous of the lady, by any chance, because she's so elegant and sirenish, are you?" Ellin giggled.

"Don't be sil'," Jane smiled. "If I'm jealous of anyone, it's your own mother, Ellin Dwyer. I'd give anything to look exactly like her. I've always wished that I were a beautiful blonde."

"Everyone says that I look exactly like Mother," Ellin said with an impish grin. "But, speaking of our guest again, as we shouldn't, I think I know what you mean, Janie, and I sort of feel the same way. Somehow, I can't imagine her ever being a schoolteacher, can you?"

"No. I wonder where she taught."

"I asked her. And she was sort of vague, but she did mention some school in London. I can't remember the name."

"She's not one bit like our Paul. He's grand, isn't he?" Jane's eyes glowed. "I like him better than ever before."

"So does Milly!" Ellin chuckled. "She can't keep her eyes away from him. Look at her now! She's listening to Mother talk but she's watching Paul."

"I think he likes her, too," Jane said, suddenly serious. "They'd make a great pair, Ellin. I just discovered something."

"What?"

"Milly's *really* good-looking."

"Sure she is, when she's around Paul and all flushed and sort of trilly," Ellin agreed and laughed.

"You know, I've had such a good time today that I've almost forgotten poor, sick Miss Ramsdell and Henry," Jane said, looking up into the blue sky.

"Well, don't think about them now," Ellin advised. "As Mr. Berthon said, let's try to forget about the school and all our worries until Monday morning."

Before Jane could speak, Mrs. Dwyer called to them to run into the house and dress. The sun was beginning to sink and a chill was creeping into the air.

Dinner that evening was gay and delicious. Jane and Ellin ate with the appetites of healthy schoolgirls, but they managed to keep watchful eyes on the lean handsomeness of Mr. Berthon, who surprised even them by the witty brilliance of his conversation. Lucienne smiled and maintained her lazy, listening, but charming, silence. Miss Brand sparkled and glowed and looked lovelier than ever.

The talk drifted brightly from subject to subject, and finally, to Holly Hall. Then a serious note entered into the voices.

"To me, the sudden departure of Henry is even stranger

than the theft of Miss Ramsdell's jewelry," Mrs. Dwyer
said quietly. "Miss Brand tells me that Henry had been
at the school for fifteen years! I can't imagine why he
would walk out that way in the night."

"No one can understand it," Miss Brand said seriously.

"His race has wandering feet,-so I'm told," Mr. Berthon
remarked. "Perhaps he just suddenly grew tired of school-
teachers and schoolgirls and decided to try new fields. Or
perhaps he was involved in some local romance he
couldn't break off in any other way."

"Not Henry." Miss Brand shook her smooth, shining
head. "In all the years I've known him, he has never had
a 'girl,' in spite of all the good-looking colored maids in
the neighborhood. Miss Ramsdell used to wish that he
would find someone and settle down. She even offered
him that little cottage back of the garages, if he'd marry.
But Henry just wasn't interested in girls."

Quickly Jane looked at Mr. Berthon, but he was watching Miss Brand. So, Jane thought, Henry had been meeting girls on the sly, slipping home late at night, when
Miss Ramsdell thought he was sleeping in the garage.
Perhaps Mr. Berthon was right. Perhaps Henry had been
"mixed up" in some kind of a romance. That might explain his sudden disappearance, which had so shocked
and worried the school.

"You don't suppose that Henry's leaving could have
had anything to do with the stealing of Miss Ramsdell's
jewelry, do you?" Mr. Dwyer asked thoughtfully a few

minutes later, when they were drinking their after-dinner coffee in the long, softly-lighted living room.

"I don't think so," Miss Brand answered quickly. "Henry was as honest as the day is long."

"Speaking of jewels, Mother has some heirlooms, too, haven't you, Mum?" Ellin asked brightly.

"They're really your father's heirlooms."

Margaret Dwyer smiled at her daughter. Then she turned to the others and explained:

"They've been passed down for several generations to the wives of the oldest Dwyer sons."

"Oh, yes, the famous Dwyer rubies!" Miss Brand exclaimed. "I remember reading about them in some newspaper story about well-known jewel collections. They must be exquisite."

"I'd love to see them sometime," Jane cried enthusiastically.

"You can see them tonight, if you'd like," Mrs. Dwyer told them. "They happen to be here in the house. Usually I keep them in the bank in town, but I brought them out from New York yesterday to wear to the charity ball next week. It's an annual affair and we make quite a big thing of it out here."

"I'm like Jane," Miss Brand smiled. "I'd love to see them. Rubies are my favorites of all precious stones."

"I like them best, too, I believe," Lucienne Berthon said quietly.

"Shall I get them for you, Margaret?" Mr. Dwyer asked, rising from his chair.

"They're not in the big safe in the library, Hugh," Mrs. Dwyer told him. "I put them in the small safe in my sitting room. So I'll get them. " She walked lightly toward the door. "Hugh doesn't know the combination of my safe. That's where I keep all my secrets," she said as she laughed over her shoulder. "I even hide the slip of paper with the combination on it."

A few moments later Lucienne stood up languidly and moved slowly toward the door through which Mrs. Dwyer had disappeared.

"I'll run upstairs and get a wrap before Mrs. Dwyer returns," she said in explanation. "The days are very warm but the evenings grow cool."

"Shall we close the windows?" Mr. Dwyer asked quickly.

"No. No, I love the smell of Autumn in the air. But this dress is very thin." She touched the shoulder of her white crepe gown.

Ellin jumped to her feet. "May I get your wrap for you?"

"Thank you, my dear. But I think it is still in my bag, probably in the very bottom. I had better hunt for it, myself." She smiled and disappeared in the wake of Mrs. Dwyer.

She returned in a short time with Mrs. Dwyer. Lucienne was wearing a loose silk coat of lime green over her white gown and Mrs. Dwyer carried several pearl-gray velvet cases.

She put the cases down on a table and the others quickly gathered around her.

"The cases themselves are heirlooms, too, aren't they?" Mr. Berthon asked, lightly touching one of the carved gold clasps.

"Yes, they're as old as the rubies," Mr. Dwyer answered.

Then Mrs. Dwyer opened the cases, one by one, and everyone, even the languid Lucienne, uttered small, involuntary cries of admiration.

The flawless rubies glowed against the dull grey satin of the cases' lining. There were two necklaces, a tiara, four bracelets, three pins and, in smaller cases, four priceless pairs of earrings and three handsome finger rings.

"My great-great-grandfather started the collection and each generation has added to it," Mr. Dwyer explained. "Our contribution, so far, has been this pin and this ring." He pointed to an exquisite bar of the gleaming stones and one perfect ruby, set in a ring. "As you see, the jewelers duplicated the original settings."

"And they duplicated the cases, too," Mr. Berthon added.

"They're beautiful!" Jane cried breathlessly. "No wonder people talk about the famous Dwyer rubies!"

"Lovely," Lucienne Berthon sighed. "Simply lovely!"

"They are beautiful," Margaret Dwyer agreed simply. "I am very, very proud of them. And, since we have no

The Flawless Rubies Glowed in Their Cases

son, they will be Ellin's some day."

Mr. Berthon picked up a ring from one of the small cases and examined it carefully.

"It looks absolutely flawless," he said admiringly. "Of course, I am no connoisseur of rubies, but it seems perfect to me."

"I don't know much about jewelry either, but they tell me all the stones are perfect," Mr. Dwyer said with quiet pride. "There are far larger collections of rubies in this country, I understand, but jewelers tell me that there are no flawed stones among these."

"Put them away, Mrs. Dwyer, before I eat them," Jane cried laughingly. "I didn't know that any stones could be as beautiful as these are. They look almost as if they were alive."

When the cases were closed, Mrs. Dwyer and Ellin carried them back to their place in the wall safe in Mrs. Dwyer's upstairs sitting room. Then they returned to their guests, and the conversation gradually veered from jewels and famous jewel collections to games and sports.

It was when the guests were leaving the next evening, Lucienne to return by train to New York and the others by car to Holly Hall, that the rubies were mentioned again. It had been a long, lazy sunny Sunday. While the others played tennis after luncheon, Lucienne had wandered in the gardens. And at dinner she had shown more animation than ever before.

Then, as they were saying good-bye later, she said, "I

want to thank you again for allowing us to see those exquisite jewels, Mrs. Dwyer. It was a real privilege and I appreciate it. I know that you will be beautiful when you wear them at the party."

"When does this charity ball take place?" Mr. Berthon asked.

"Thursday night," Mrs. Dwyer told him, then added with a little shiver, "I'll confess that I'll be glad when Friday comes and I can return the rubies to the bank. I always feel uneasy when they're left in the house for any length of time."

"That's ridiculous, Margaret." Mr. Dwyer put his arm affectionately around his wife's slender shoulders. "They're just as safe here as they are in the bank. Besides, what would anyone do with them? They couldn't dispose of them in this country. They're too well-known."

"I hope you're right, Hugh," she sighed.

"It has been a perfect week-end," Mr. Berthon said as they walked toward the car. "Now I hope that all of you will visit Lucienne and me in our little cottage. We're there always on Sunday and the latch-string, as you put it, is always out."

"You may be sorry you issued that general invitation, Mr. Berthon." Ellin's eyes twinkled. "You and Miss Berthon may be seeing Miss Brand and Jane and me more often than you wish."

"It couldn't be too often," Lucienne Berthon said with one of her slow, indolent smiles. Turning to Mrs. Dwyer, she added, "The week-end has been wonderful. You will never know what it has meant to Paul and me."

Afterward, Jane remembered those words and wondered.

CHAPTER SIX

MYSTERY AFTER MYSTERY

The following week Holly Hall returned to almost normal calm. Again Miss Abigail appeared at the faculty table, but her slender body was not as straight as it had been and her steps faltered now and then. Their days were so filled with study and play that the girls talked less and less about the lost or stolen jewelry. Even Jane and Ellin forgot that somewhere, somehow, a secret investigation into the mystery was still being made.

A new, brown-skinned chauffeur came to take Henry's place and to wear the dignified, gray uniform of the school. So even Henry's strange disappearance gradually ceased to be the subject of whisperings and wonderings.

The only interest which did not wane was the excitement caused by Paul Berthon. The girls still rushed eagerly to his classes, still made all kinds of excuses to talk to him, still watched him covertly from the corners of their eyes as he sat at the faculty table.

Then, on Friday evening, Jane and Ellin were jerked brusquely from the peaceful serenity of the study hour by a telephone call for Ellin.

When she returned to the room, her brown eyes were wide with dismay and her round face looked pinched and pale.

"Ellin! What in the world is the matter?" Jane exclaimed, jumping up from her chair.

"It was Mother," Ellin answered in a choked voice. "The rubies have been stolen!"

"The *rubies!* Stolen?" Jane repeated, unable to believe Ellin's words. "How? When?"

Ellin sank down in a crumpled heap on her bed. "Last night or early this morning," she said forlornly.

"How did it happen? Who stole them?" Jane cried.

"No one knows," Ellin answered in a dull voice. "Mother is simply stunned. Of course, they are covered by insurance, but you know how proud Mother and Dad were of those perfect rubies. No others could ever take their place."

"Yes, I know," Jane said slowly. "Tell me about it. What did your Mother say?"

"Mother wore some of them to the big party last night. When she came home, she put them back in their little cases and locked them in her little safe. Dad and she both distinctly remember counting the cases and making sure that they were all there. Also they remember closing and locking the safe. They had an engagement tonight in New York, so Mother decided to leave early and take the rubies back to the bank. When she opened the safe this afternoon to get them, they were gone."

"Was the safe broken?"

"No. It was opened by someone who either knew the

combination or figured it out. There are crooks who can find out combinations by feeling the locks, or something, aren't there?"

"I don't know. I guess so. But maybe the thief found the paper with the combination written on it," Jane suggested.

"I don't think so. It was where Mother always hid it, in an old envelope in her desk in her sitting room. And nothing was disturbed."

"How did the thief get into the house?"

"That's another thing the police can't figure out, Mother said. All the doors and windows were locked from the inside, just as they were left the night before. All the servants testified to that. The police have been questioning them all day. But no one heard or saw anything out of the ordinary. The night watchman made his rounds regularly all night and he didn't see even a pinpoint of light in the house, after Mother and Dad came home and went to bed. The police think it must have been done between two in the morning, when Mother and Dad went to sleep, and six o'clock, when the cook and the houseman came down from their room on the third floor."

"Is there anything we can do?" Jane asked anxiously. "I can't bear to sit still here at school and not do *anything.*"

"Mother said that the police may want to question us and everyone who has been a guest at the house recently.

That would mean Miss Brand and Mr. and Miss Berthon. They think we might have seen or heard something which would be a clue, I guess. Mother'll call us, if they want us to go home."

"Let's tell Miss Brand about it now," Jane suggested quickly. "She admired the rubies so much and she's so smart. Maybe she will be able to remember something."

"We might tell Mr. Berthon, too, if he's staying in Faculty Cottage tonight," Ellin added.

The girls slipped through the deserted halls and down the stairs. But, as they opened the front doors and started down the steps to the lawn, the school's night watchman stopped them.

"Where you young ladies goin'?" he asked sharply.

He was a grizzled, gray lump of a man, who had been guarding the school for years.

"We have a message for Miss Brand in Faculty Cottage," Jane explained hastily.

"Sure about that?" he asked suspiciously. "It's against orders for young ladies to be wanderin' around the grounds at this hour of the night."

"But we're not wandering," Jane insisted. "We're going to Faculty Cottage. Come with us, Mr. Gridley, if you don't believe us. Miss Brand will tell you that it's all right, when she hears our message."

So, accompanied by the still doubtful Mr. Gridley, the girls hurried across the lawn to Faculty Cottage. The watchman followed them into the building and up the stairs to the women's section and down the hall to Miss Brand's apartment.

Jane knocked briskly on the door. There was no answer. Again she knocked—still no answer.

"She's not in, I guess," she said finally.

"Let's try Mr. Berthon's apartment," Ellin suggested.

"You young ladies ain't allowed in the men's section, except by special permission," Mr. Gridley reminded them.

"It will be all right, if you come with us," Jane said sweetly. "And Mr. Berthon will take the responsibility, I know. The message is very important."

So Mr. Gridley, grumbling loudly, followed them down the stairs to Mr. Berthon's apartment.

Again they knocked and again there was no response.

"Well, I guess your important message'll have to keep till mornin'," the watchman said grimly. "I'll see you safely back to the Hall."

As they walked down the steps of the Cottage, they met Dr. Cornelia Stratton and Miss Mercer, also of the Psychology Department. They were evidently returning from the library, because their arms were piled high with books.

"Good evening, young ladies." Dr. Stratton frowned behind her spectacles. "What are you doing here at this hour?"

"We had a very important message for Miss Brand," Jane answered politely. "Mr. Gridley came with us to make sure that Miss Brand approved."

"Well, you won't find Miss Brand here tonight," Dr. Stratton informed them. "She has gone out for the evening."

"Since Miss Brand isn't here, do you know where we could find Mr. Berthon?" Jane asked with her best smile.

"Mr. Berthon and Miss Brand have gone to the village to the movies," Miss Mercer said unexpectedly, then bit her lip.

Miss Mercer had been at Holly Hall only ten years. Dr. Stratton did not speak, but the scowl which she turned upon Miss Mercer was a stronger reprimand than any words could have been.

"Take the young ladies back to the Hall, Gridley," she ordered. "I am sure that your message can wait until morning. Good night."

"Yes'm," Jane and Ellin murmured in wilted voices and followed the bulk of Gridley back to the Hall.

"Cornelia's jealous of our Milly and Paul," Ellin whispered, when they were safely back in their own room.

"Milly must be making progress." Jane smiled knowingly. "I'll bet it's their first date, Ellin."

Then they remembered the stolen rubies and forgot about romance.

"We'll tell them the first thing in the morning," Jane said. "They'll probably have to go with us, if we go to your house for questioning."

But the next morning they knew that they wouldn't

have to tell Miss Brand and Mr. Berthon about the theft of the rubies. The story was blazoned in headlines in the morning newspapers. Miss Brand herself brought the paper to their room before breakfast.

"I can't tell you how sorry I am, Ellin," Miss Brand said, her clear eyes clouded. "I know what this loss must mean to your Mother and Father."

Jane, who was eagerly reading the newspaper story, suddenly cried, "It says here, 'This is the fifth large jewel robbery in six weeks. It is suspected that the thefts must be the work of a syndicate of criminals, with spies working in the homes of the victims, since all the cases show an intimate knowledge of the habits of the families.' "

"Yes," Miss Brand commented quietly. "Someone inside your house must have learned the combination of the safe, Ellin, since it was opened so quietly and efficiently. Do you think it could possibly be one of the servants?"

"Mother says absolutely not," Ellen answered. "The cook and her husband—he's the houseman—have been with us for years. So have the two maids. The chauffeur came to us about two years ago, but Mother says that she would trust him with anything. The two gardeners are fairly new, but they worked for friends of ours for years. Besides, they live in a little cottage of their own and never come near the house. Mother said that, when the police questioned all of them yesterday, you could tell just by looking at their faces that they were innocent."

"Is there anything I can do?" Miss Brand asked.

Jane Eagerly Read the Newspaper

"You'll probably have to answer a lot of questions. All of us will. They're going to talk to everyone who's been in the house during the last few weeks, Mother said."

"I wonder what Mr. Berthon and his sister will say, when they read about it," Jane said, folding the newspaper. "We tried to find you and Mr. Berthon last night, Miss Brand, but you both were away."

Miss Brand's cheeks flushed and her eyes glowed.

"Mr. Berthon invited me to go to see a motion picture in the village," she said. "Then he brought me back to the school and went on to his cottage, the one he has up the road. He said that his sister would be arriving this evening."

"Don't you think it would be a good plan for the three of us to go to his house this morning and talk to him?" Jane's voice was eager. "He might have some ideas."

"Do you think Miss Ramsdell would give us permission to go, if you went with us, Miss Brand?" Ellin added. "It's Saturday morning and we haven't any classes except physical education."

"I'll ask Miss Ramsdell," Miss Brand promised after a brief pause. "Come, girls. There's the breakfast gong."

Since the faculty table usually had several vacancies at Saturday breakfast, Miss Brand moved into Mr. Berthon's empty chair beside Miss Abigail. From their table Jane and Ellin could see her talking quietly to the Head Mistress. Then she looked toward them and nodded.

"We can go!" Jane exclaimed happily.

Bunny Walters and Mary Lou, who had been busily asking questions about the exciting events at the Dwyer home, looked up in surprise.

"Go where?" they chorused.

"That's a secret," Jane laughed mysteriously. "You girls are too young to know. Someday we'll tell you, maybe."

Miss Brand waited for Jane and Ellin in the hall after breakfast.

"Miss Ramsdell has given us permission to go immediately after lunch," she told them. "She doesn't want you to miss your morning classes."

So, early that afternoon, Jane and Ellin were rolling along the shore road in the station wagon, with Miss Brand at the wheel. It was a crisp, cool day, with a soft purplish haze over the river and the opposite bank. Indian summer had departed and autumn had arrived with all its vivid reds and oranges.

"Do you know where Mr. Berthon's house is, Miss Brand?" Ellin asked, nudging Jane.

"Not exactly," Miss Brand answered calmly. "But I think I'll know it when I see it.

They drove in silence for awhile and then Miss Brand exclaimed suddenly, "There it is! That picturesque little cottage."

"It looks like the kind of house Mr. Berthon would like," Jane cried with young enthusaism. "Sort of old-worldish."

It was a small, two-storied English cottage, built of gray

field stone, and it nestled in a little hollow between two tree-covered knolls. Its low-hanging eaves and diamond-paned windows gave it a quaint, story-book air, as if it had stepped from the pages of a fairy tale or an old romance. A winding, gravel driveway led from the main road to the front stoop of flat stones and a wide oak door formed the entrance to the house.

"He's home," Ellin said as Miss Brand stopped the car in the driveway.

She pointed to a pillar of smoke, rising from the huge, stone chimney.

Mr. Berthon opened the door before they could lift the heavy knocker.

"I heard your car," he said after he had greeted them. He was smiling, but Jane was startled by the grim coldness of his eyes. *"He looks as if he were afraid, or very angry,"* she thought.

"We came to tell you about—," Miss Brand began, but she did not finish the sentence.

"The theft of Mrs. Dwyer's rubies," Mr. Berthon interrupted almost savagely. "I saw a paper this morning, when I drove into the village to buy supplies. I was shocked when I read about it, and angry, too. I phoned your mother immediately, Ellin, and offered any help I could give. I know how your Mother and Father must feel."

He ushered them into a stone-floored hall, then through wide doors into a long, beamed living room, with a bright fire blazing in a huge stone fireplace at one end of the room.

As they stepped through the doors, Lucienne Berthon arose from a low couch and came forward to meet them.

"Miss Berthon!" Jane exclaimed, surprised, and disappointed, for she had hoped that they would find Mr. Berthon alone.

"Yes, I'm here," Lucienne said without her usual smile. "As soon as I saw the papers this morning, I made arrangements to leave the shop and take the first train up here. I was terribly upset by the news."

"It seems incredible that one of the servants, whom your family trusted so implicitly, could have done such a thing. And yet there seems no other explanation," Mr. Berthon said, when they were sitting in comfortable chairs near the hearth and he had added another log to the blaze.

"I don't think any of the servants had anything to do with it," Ellin stated with firm conviction.

"But how else could it have been done?" Lucienne asked, lighting a cigarette. "Someone knew exactly where your mother kept the rubies and the safe's combination, knew everything about the house. Nothing was disturbed. If one of the servants didn't actually take the rubies, he, or she, must have helped, at least."

"I'll never believe that they had anything to do with it," Ellin repeated with young firmness.

"You are very sure of them, aren't you?" Mr. Berthon

asked quietly.

"Absolutely. And so are Mother and Dad."

"Your Mother said the police might want to ask us some questions, since we were guests in your home so recently," Mr. Berthon went on. "Lucienne and I have been wracking our brains, trying to remember any little incident which might be of interest to the investigators. But we can think of nothing."

"Neither can we," Jane said.

"Well," Lucienne said slowly and smiled, "I think there is nothing we can do about it, except wait to be called by the police, if they intend to call us."

There was a crunching of gravel, as a car turned into the driveway. A moment later the knocker of the door was pounded heavily.

CHAPTER SEVEN

SOMETHING CONCEALED?

Paul Berthon opened the door and faced two strange men, one tall and thin with mild, faded eyes, the other shorter and thinner with a sharp, pointed face.

"You Paul Berthon?" the first one asked in a quiet voice.

"Yes."

"Well, I'm Matthews and this is Drake. We're investigators from the Albermarle Insurance Company. We'd like to talk to you and your sister, if she's here."

Matthews handed Paul a card in a cellophane case, stating that he was Ward Matthews, special investigator.

"Come in, gentlemen," Mr. Berthon invited courteously and led the two newcomers into the living room, where he introduced them to the others.

"Just want to ask a few questions about the Dwyer rubies. Routine, you know," Matthews explained affably, while Drake surveyed the room with silent indifference.

"We'll be glad to answer any questions you care to ask," Mr. Berthon said, smiling. "But I'm afraid we won't be much help to you."

"Maybe you'll be more help than you think." Matthews' tones were mild, like his pale eyes.

"We saw the rubies, you know, a few days before they

were stolen," Lucienne volunteered. "They were lovely."
She sighed.

"Yes. Heard about that," Matthews said briefly, flicking his gaze from Lucienne's relaxed, graceful body in its dark blue slacks to Miss Brand's erect, gray-tweed alertness.

"We were all together when Mrs. Dwyer showed us the rubies," Miss Brand added in her clear voice.

"So I was told. Lucky we found you here. Saves time." Matthews turned from Miss Brand to Jane and Ellin, who sat, side by side, on a divan. "Which one of you girls is Ellin Dwyer?"

"I am," Ellin answered quickly.

"Thought so." Matthews smiled. "Look like your Mother. You can run along, if you want to. And you, too, Miss," he added, looking at Jane. "Your folks asked us not to disturb you two girls, unless it was necessary."

"But we'd like to stay, wouldn't we, Jane?" Ellin asked quickly.

"Yes," Jane replied. "Maybe we can be of some help, Mr. Matthews."

"Okay," Matthews agreed. "We'll ask you two a few questions first. Just to get the records straight, you understand. One of you tell me what you've been doing since you left the Dwyer house Sunday evening."

"We drove straight back to the school, after we stopped at the Hollytown station to put Miss Berthon on the train for New York," Jane told him. "We haven't been away from the school grounds since, except to come here today."

"Same thing go for you, Miss?" Matthews asked Ellin and she nodded.

"Have either of you had any unusual phone calls or mail, since you came back to school?"

The girls answered in one voice:

"No."

"Well, I guess that finishes you two," Matthews said. "Now you, Miss—" he consulted his notebook—"Miss Brand, is that right?"

"Yes, Millicent Brand. My story is practically the same as that of the girls. We returned together from the Dwyer home and I have remained on the school grounds until last evening, when Mr. Berthon and I went into the village, Hollytown, to a motion-picture theater."

"Did you come directly home from the movies?" Matthews asked, a twinkle in his eyes as he looked at Miss Brand.

"Yes, of course," she said. Then she flushed. "I almost forgot. We stopped for a cup of coffee and a sandwich at the Village Sweet Shop, next door to the theater. Then we came directly back to the school, where Mr. Berthon left me at the door of the Faculty Cottage."

"Was Mr. Berthon with you constantly from the time you left the school until you went back again?"

It was Drake who asked the question and all the eyes turned to him, startled by the sudden raspy sound of his

Matthews Questioned Each of Them in Turn

voice.

"Yes. No. Let me think," Miss Brand faltered. "I remember now. He excused himself for a moment. Said that he wanted to make a phone call to his sister about their plans for the week-end. He went into a telephone booth in the rear of the shop. But he was gone only a very short time."

"And that's the only time he was away from you during the evening?" Drake spoke again.

"Yes," Miss Brand answered without hesitation.

"About mail and telephone calls during the past week, have you received anything out of the ordinary?"

Matthews was doing the questioning again and Drake retired into his silence.

"Nothing unusual."

"Did Berthon say he talked to his sister, when he came back after making that phone call?" Drake asked the question without moving his gaze from the hand-hewn beams of the ceiling.

"Yes, I believe he did," Miss Brand replied after a moment's thought. "I'm sure he did. He said that Lucienne, that's Miss Berthon, would come up on the eight o'clock train after her shop closed, and he suggested that I might bring the girls for tea on Sunday afternoon."

"Do you happen to remember what time Berthon made that phone call?" Drake asked next.

"Yes, I do, because I looked at my watch while Mr. Berthon was gone," Miss Brand replied. "We are supposed to be back at the school by twelve and I was a little worried about the time. It was exactly ten minutes after eleven."

"Is that right, Berthon?" Matthews interrupted suddenly.

"It must be, since Miss Brand looked at her watch." Mr. Berthon smiled pleasantly as he said this.

"Why did you call your sister at that time of night? Any special reason?" Matthews persisted.

"None at all. I always call her on Friday evenings to learn her plans for the week-end. Sometimes she is able to leave early, and sometimes late, on Saturdays. I like to know so that I can meet her train."

"And, when you talked to her last night, she said that it would be late today?"

"Yes. She changed her plans, when she read the news about the robbery in the morning paper."

"*Why?*"

The one word cracked like a pistol shot from Drake's mouth and he pulled his eyes from the ceiling to stare at Lucienne.

But neither his question nor his stare disturbed Lucienne's calm.

"Why did I change my plans?" she said serenely, smiling straight into Drake's gaze. "Because I was upset by the news. I wanted to be with my brother."

"Why should the news upset you so much?" Drake snapped. "You are not an intimate friend of the Dwyers, are you? Robberies, of one kind or another, take place every day. They don't upset you, do they?"

"Certainly not, Mr. Drake." Lucienne's voice was sweetly indulgent, almost as if she were placating an unreasonable, and not very intelligent, customer. "Please remember that I was a guest in the Dwyer home less than a week ago, that I saw, and even touched, the famous rubies. Also you must please not forget that my brother is in daily contact with the daughter of the family. I can't see that there is anything unusual about my feelings. It seems to me that any normal person would have felt the same way, under the same circumstances."

Drake shrugged his shoulders and returned to his silent study of the ceiling beams.

"Please tell me briefly what you have been doing this past week, Mr. Berthon," Matthews requested mildly.

"I returned to the school with Miss Brand and the young ladies. Until last evening, when, as Miss Brand told you, we went to the theater, I have remained at the school. After taking Miss Brand home last evening, I came directly here and went to bed. This morning I drove into the village to buy supplies for the week-end, as I do every Saturday. After reading the shocking news in the paper, I phoned Mrs. Dwyer. Then I returned here, and here I have been ever since."

"You did not meet your sister's train this morning?"

"No. I didn't know that she was coming. She drove from the station in the local taxicab."

"Why didn't you phone your sister, when you called Mrs. Dwyer?" This was Drake.

"I tried to do so," Mr. Berthon replied pleasantly. "She had left her apartment and had not yet arrived at the shop."

"Have you received any unusual mail or phone calls this week?" This was Matthews.

"No. Not even usual ones. I have few friends in this country, Mr. Matthews, and the mail from Europe is very irregular now."

"I see." Matthews nodded and turned to Lucienne.

"It is my turn now, is it not?" She smiled and spoke, before he could ask his first question. "Sunday night I returned by train to New York and took a taxi to my apartment. I was at the shop every day from nine in the morning until six in the evening. Except today. I went to the shop about nine-thirty this morning. I was later than usual, because I stopped to read the paper. I made arrangements to leave immediately and took the ten-fifteen train to come up here."

"And the evenings, Miss Berthon?"

Matthews idly flipped the pages of his notebook as he awaited her reply.

Briefly, and without hesitation, Lucienne outlined her activities of the five evenings. Monday, Tuesday and Wednesday she had had dinner at a small restaurant near her apartment house, then had gone home and spent the evening, resting and reading. Thursday she had had dinner with a friend, a Mr. H. G. Gilbert. They had gone to a theater. Friday she had worked late at the shop. She had eaten a sandwich in a drugstore, then gone home.

"My life is very simple," she said in conclusion. "I have few friends. I have received no personal mail this week and no phone calls, except from my brother and Mr. Gilbert."

"You don't mean Harry Gilbert, the race-horse man, do you?" Matthews asked, sudden interest lighting his faded eyes.

"I think he owns race horses. I understand he owns yachts, too," she answered casually.

"He owns about a dozen oil wells and half a county," Drake spoke up suddenly to say. "Has a summer place up around here somewhere. How'd you happen to meet H. G. Gilbert, Miss Berthon?"

"His daughter is one of our customers. She introduced her father to me one day."

"You may have only a few friends, but you sure pick 'em right," Drake snapped, and there was a keenly appraising admiration in the quick glance he directed toward Lucienne, before his eyes returned to the ceiling.

"And you were home Friday night, when your brother called?" Matthews asked quietly.

"Why, yes." Lucienne seemed surprised at the question. "Of course. Why do you ask?"

"Because at ten minutes after eleven, when Miss Brand

said he phoned you, I was ringing your doorbell and no one was home," Drake said sharply.

There was a brief, startled silence in the room. Jane and Ellin looked at each other with bewildered eyes.

Lucienne broke that silence by a ripple of low laughter.

"I'm sorry, Mr. Drake. If I had known it was you, I would have opened the door," she said apologetically. "I thought it was someone else. A young man who is very annoying and persistent. I had told him I would not be home. So I did not answer the doorbell."

"I see."

But Drake's voice did not sound convinced. It was weighted with suspicion and even Matthews' mild eyes had hardened.

"You rang three times, with intervals of about a half minute between rings, didn't you?" Lucienne asked indulgently.

"Yes," Drake admitted.

"Then I am sure that it was your ring I heard," Lucienne smiled. "Again I apologize."

Jane and Ellin sighed with relief and their tense bodies relaxed.

Then Mr. Berthon asked the question which had been in their minds, unspoken, for the last few minutes.

"Do you suspect my sister or me of any complicity in the Dwyer robbery?" His voice was cold as steel and his eyes were grim as they looked directly at Matthews. "If

you do, please say so. We'll be happy to prove our innocence to you. But I do not like the veiled innuendoes in
your questions, gentlemen. I resent it, both for myself
and for my sister."

"No, no, of course, not," Matthews answered hastily.
"This is just routine, Mr. Berthon. We are questioning
everyone who has been in the Dwyer home recently, as
I told you before."

"Wasn't it rather late for Mr. Drake to call at my
sister's apartment?" Paul Berthon's voice had not soft-
ened.

"Guess maybe it was," Matthews said with a conciliat-
ing smile. "He'd been there earlier, but she wasn't home.
So he went back, after he'd spent the evening checkin'
up on some business acquaintances of Mr. Dwyer who
were at the house Monday night for dinner. We ain't
missin' anybody, Berthon. He thought maybe he could
finish up with your sister the same evening. This all may
seem kinda ridiculous to you folks, but it's company
orders and we just work there, you know."

The taut muscles of Mr. Berthon's face relaxed.

"We all have to follow orders," he said quietly. "Have
you gentlemen any other questions?"

"Just this." Matthews leaned forward in his chair.
"Thinkin' back over the time you spent at the Dwyer
place, do any of you remember anything out of the
ordinary, anything at all?"

No one did.

"Didn't you think the old envelope was a very smart hiding place, when you saw Mrs. Dwyer *put the combination of the safe back in it,* Miss Berthon?"

Drake's question exploded in the room like a gunshot. Jane, Ellin, Miss Brand and Paul Berthon jumped in startled surprise. Only Lucienne remained undisturbed.

"I thought you would eventually reach that question, Mr. Drake," she said serenely. "I have been waiting for it. Why don't you come out openly, as Paul asked, and accuse me of stealing the rubies?"

"You haven't answered my question, Miss Berthon."

Drake was standing now and he was no longer looking at the ceiling. He was staring straight down at Lucienne.

"I *will* answer it," she said, meeting his gaze without a quiver. "But it will be a disappointing answer. I did not see Mrs. Dwyer take out or put back anything, not even the rubies. I knew nothing about any envelope until I read this morning's paper."

"You were upstairs when Mrs. Dwyer was getting the rubies."

There was open accusation now in Drake's voice and he had dropped his indifference.

"Of course, I was. That's no secret. Everyone saw me go upstairs and everyone saw me return. But Mrs. Dwyer will tell you, I am sure, that I did not enter her room. I went directly to my own room to get my wrap."

"You passed the door, didn't you?"

"You Haven't Answered My Question."

"Certainly. But it was closed."

"We have only your word for that."

"You can ask Mrs. Dwyer."

"I did," Drake snapped. "Mrs. Dwyer said that she was sure that she had left her bedroom door open. She remembers because, when she came back with the rubies, both hands were filled and she did not have to open any door."

"That's right," Again Lucienne spoke calmly, while Jane and Ellin held their breaths in excited suspense. "The bedroom door was open. I know, because I met Mrs. Dwyer just as she came out with the jewels and we went downstairs together."

"Then why did you say just now that it was closed?" Drake barked.

"I wasn't speaking of the bedroom door. I meant the sitting-room door. The safe is in the sitting room. The two rooms connect and Mrs. Dwyer walked through her bedroom into her sitting room, evidently. When I went upstairs, I noticed that the bedroom door was open, but I did not see Mrs. Dwyer so I knew that she must be in the sitting room."

"The sitting room has a door opening into the hall, too," Drake pointed out.

"I know. Next to the bedroom door. But it was closed. I am positive of that."

Drake swung toward Ellin.

"If the sitting-room door was closed, as Miss Berthon

says, could she have looked into the sitting room through the bedroom door?" he asked quickly.

"No, I don't think so," Ellin replied, her voice shaking with excitement. "And I'm sure, too, that the sitting room door was closed, Mr. Drake. It was, when I went upstairs to help Mother put the rubies away. We walked through the bedroom. And I'm positive no one could see the desk where Mother keeps the combination, from the hall. It's on a corner of the sitting room." The words tumbled out in a breathless haste.

"All right. All right!" Drake cried and he seemed to wilt before their eyes. "I'll check on all this and, if I've made a mistake, I apologize, Miss Berthon. Come on, Matthews, let's get going."

The two men strode across the room. At the door Matthews paused and turned.

"We all make mistakes, folks," he said in his mild voice. "Sorry about this one. Hope you'll forget it."

Mr. Berthon followed them to the door and closed it behind them. When he came back into the room, his face was pale and set.

"Oh, I'm so sorry that this happened, Miss Berthon and Mr. Berthon," Ellin cried, tears in her brown eyes. "Mother and Dad will be terribly upset about it."

"I don't suppose we can blame them, really," Mr. Berthon said thoughtfully. "After all, Lucienne and I are practically strangers and Lucienne did go upstairs at the time that Mrs. Dwyer was getting the rubies. I can see how they might suspect—"

"It's ridiculous! Utterly ridiculous!" Ellin's eyes blazed with anger.

"Well, let's forget about it," Mr. Berthon smiled suddenly.

With that smile, the tension in the room relaxed. Jane sighed and Miss Brand leaned back in her chair.

"I think we're all ready for a cup of tea, after that ordeal," Lucienne laughed lightly. She walked to Ellin and patted the girl's shoulder gently. "Don't worry, my dear child. They had to suspect someone and I was the logical one. Now I'll fix tea."

"Your mother'll prove to that horrible Drake how wrong he was," Jane said, patting Ellin's clenched fingers. "And now maybe Mr. Berthon will show us around this ducky little house. I'm dying to see it, aren't you, Miss Brand?"

Miss Brand nodded.

So Mr. Berthon led them on a tour of inspection through the quaint rooms of the old house. Gradually, as they walked and talked, the strain of the last half hour died away, and, when they returned to the living room, they were laughing normally.

"The cottage was built by an artist, I understand," Mr. Berthon said. "That explains the queer shapes and sizes of the rooms and the different floor levels, I imagine."

"Where does that door go?" Ellin asked. pointing to a heavy oak door at the end of the room. "Does that lead into another funny little room?"

"No." Mr. Berthon opened the door and they saw a deep closet, filled with coats, hanging on hangers, and odds and ends of trunks and luggage. "It's a sort of catch-everything closet," he explained. "Whenever we can't find a place for something, we put it in here. Now, if you'd like to see the garden, we'll go outside. Lucienne and I are very proud of our little garden. We take care of it, ourselves."

He closed the closet door and led the way outside.

Jane and Ellin exclaimed enthusiastically over the charm of the garden, with its autumn flowers and richly colored leaves. The stone cottage snuggled down in the shrubbery, as if it, too, had grown there. Chattering gaily, the four walked along the flagstone paths which follow-ed the irregular outlines of the house.

"Look! Here's another room! Which one is this, Mr. Berthon?" Jane asked.

It was just as they turned a corner and saw a small, square, one-storied ell, half-buried in still-green shrub-bery. Its two windows were closed and shrouded in heavy draperies.

"That's the storeroom," Mr. Berthon explained. "I im-agine the artist designed it to store his canvases and working materials. But we just use it for books. There's Lucienne looking for us. Tea's ready."

Back in the living room, the unseen presences of Matthews and Drake seemed to hover over the tea table.

The carefree gaiety which they had known in the garden was gone. They deliberately talked of casual things, avoiding all mention of the one subject which filled their minds. After she had performed her duties as hostess, Lucienne returned to her usual smiling silence and the others gravely discussed Holly Hall.

Jane sipped her tea and snuggled deeply into her big arm chair at one corner of the hearth. Suddenly, as she moved, the spoon slipped from her saucer and slid into the crevice between the chair's cushion and the padded arm. Jane reached down to retrieve it. As her slender fingers slid down into the crevice, they touched something under the spoon, something soft and small and square.

Cautiously she pulled it up and looked down at it.

It was one of the small gray boxes, which she had last seen in the Dwyer living room and which had held a ring, set with a glowing ruby.

CHAPTER EIGHT

A PROWLER BY NIGHT

No one heard Jane's stifled gasp.

Quickly she dropped her napkin over the gray velvet case and took a deep gulp of tea to try to still the cold trembling of her body.

One of the Dwyer jewel cases, here in Paul Berthon's living room! She couldn't believe it. It simply couldn't be true.

For a moment she almost cried out her shocked surprise. But something suppressed the words on her lips. She must think quietly and clearly.

She looked quickly at the others. They weren't paying any attention to her. Ellin was talking with a seriousness which was unusual for her, telling a story which proved the complete loyalty of Henry to Miss Abigail. Evidently they were still talking about Holly Hall. Paul Berthon was listening with a smiling interest. Lucienne was listening, too, although she was gazing sleepily into the glowing flames of the fire. Miss Brand was watching Paul Berthon.

Swiftly and cautiously Jane pulled the small velvet case from the crevice of the chair and thrust it deep into her handbag, which was tucked into the chair beside her.

She felt numbed, stunned. All she wanted to do was

to get away from that house so she could think.

"Why so silent, Janie?" Ellin asked suddenly, turning toward her.

Jane could feel the others looking at her and, when she spoke, her voice sounded queerly strained, a stranger's voice. But the others didn't seem to notice it.

"I didn't have a chance to talk, while you were holding the floor, Ellin," she said, forcing a laugh.

"I guess you're right," Ellin smiled good-humoredly. "Well, I'm through. It's your turn now."

Miss Brand saved Jane by putting down her tea cup and standing.

"The tea was delicious, Miss Berthon," she said. "And I think we'd better be on our way, girls. We don't want to over-stay our welcome."

Jane sighed with relief as she, too, arose, clutching her handbag with its secret burden.

Somehow she got through the farewells to Miss Berthon, but Mr. Berthon walked with them to the car.

"We certainly have had our quota of worry and excitement these last few days, with Miss Ramsdell's loss and now the theft of the rubies," he said soberly, as he assisted Miss Brand into the seat of the station wagon.

"I hadn't intended to mention the Holly Hall robbery again," Miss Brand replied in a low voice. "But I have been wondering, Mr. Berthon, if you have noticed the similarity between the two cases. Of course, there is no similarity between the values of the stolen jewels. Miss

Ramsdell's heirlooms were very valuable but the rubies were worth a small fortune. But, with the two robberies happening so closely together and with the same efficiency and quietness, I can't keep from wondering whether the same person, or persons, might have done both."

"There's a possibility of that," Mr. Berthon nodded, his handsome face frowning in thought. "I hadn't thought of it before."

Jane hadn't thought of it before, either. But now she did, bitterly and silently.

Finally Mr. Berthon said good-bye and Jane sank down in a corner of the seat beside Ellin, while Miss Brand piloted the station wagon down the driveway.

"What's the matter, Janie? You look sick," Ellin said, looking at the silent, pale Jane.

"I'm not sick, though," Jane said briefly. "That tea was awfully strong."

"I think it's the excitement, not the tea, Jane," Miss Brand said over her shoulder. "I feel a little squeamish, myself."

"It was just like a detective story," Ellin cried. "The five of us sitting in a row, while Sherlock Matthews and his ferret-faced pal shot questions at us. It was terrible, the way they talked to Miss Berthon, wasn't it? Mother will be furious when she hears about it."

"I admired Mr. Berthon and his sister very much for the way they handled a very trying situation," Miss Brand said.

"Have You Noticed How Alike the Two Cases Are?"

"I'll never forget that Drake's face, when we proved to him that Miss Berthon couldn't possibly have seen Mother in the sitting room with the door closed," Ellin said with a little laugh.

"It's no laughing matter, Ellin," Miss Brand reminded her gravely.

No, Jane thought, it certainly was no laughing matter. The whole school would be upset, and Miss Ramsdell would probably collapse with the disgrace, if it were proved that Paul Berthon was a jewel thief. But it couldn't be true. There would be some explanation for the presence of that case in the chair. There *must* be.

A thousand wild thoughts raced through her aching head. The strange feeling she had had, when she first met Mr. Berthon's eyes in the dining hall that night. His midnight meeting with Henry in the shadows of the lawn and Henry's sudden disappearance. The voices, which she had thought she had heard, that other evening on the path beside the river. The crackling in the underbrush, which Mr. Berthon had said was a nocturnal animal. And now the jewel case in the chair in his own home. It all pointed to the guilt of only one person.

But it couldn't be true, she told herself dully again and again. Handsome, brilliant Paul Berthon could not be a thief. The very thought was ridiculous. Eminent professors of Romance Languages did not steal rubies.

Bunny, Mary Lou and several other girls were waiting for them on the terrace, when Miss Brand dropped them and drove on to the garage.

"Where have you been?" Bunny cried.

"Wait till you hear!" Ellin laughed triumphantly. "You'll be green with envy." She paused dramatically, then announced, "We've been having tea with Mr. Paul Berthon in his own home!"

Her words had the desired effect. The girls swooped down with excited questions. In the midst of the hubbub, Jane slipped away to her room.

Once inside, she carefully locked the door. Then slowly she drew the gray velvet case from her handbag. As she looked at it, turning it in her cold, trembling fingers, she lost her last hope that she might have been mistaken. There was no doubt that it was one of the Dwyer jewel cases, which she had examined so closely in the Dwyer living room because Mr. Dwyer had said that the cases, too, were heirlooms, like the rubies.

She opened the case. It was empty, as she had fearfully known it would be.

Clutching the case in her damp hand, she dropped down on the window seat and stared out toward the Hudson, shimmering in the late afternoon sunshine. She must think sanely and calmly and decide what to do. If she told Ellin, Ellin would insist upon telling her family immediately. Then the police and the insurance company's investigators would come swooping down upon Mr. Berthon and his sister and the school. Miss Abigail was already ill with the worry over her own loss. This new trouble would probably cause her complete collapse. If Mr. Berthon were innocent, and he must be, it would be terribly embarrassing for him, and it would probably cause his dismissal from the school—Miss Abigail was so strictly careful about the reputations of her teachers and her famous, irreproachable school.

Even if Mr. Berthon could prove his innocence beyond any doubt and it were Lucienne who was the guilty person, Mr. Berthon would suffer for his sister's crime. Miss Abigail would not allow the brother of a jewel thief to teach her carefully guarded "young ladies."

There was only one thing to do. She must talk to Mr. Berthon alone. He would probably be able to explain everything. If Lucienne were guilty, Mr. Berthon could probably straighten it out, return the jewels and send her away somewhere. Then, maybe, the whole matter could be hushed up before it reached the ears of Miss Abigail. She must find some way to see Mr. Berthon, and see him alone, before she told Ellin, or anyone, about the finding of the case.

Jane felt better, even a little excited, when she had finally made her decision. Somehow, she was sure that Mr. Berthon would be able to explain everything.

She hid the small jewel case in the toe of one of her shoes, far back in the closet. Then she carefully made her plans. Miss Brand and several other teachers were taking all the girls, who had not gone home over the week-end, to a Fall Festival Carnival in Hollytown that evening.

She distinctly remembered that, when the plans were discussed earlier in the week, Ellin had asked Mr. Berthon if he were going and that he had smilingly shaken his head and said, "No." So he would probably be at home that evening.

Jane decided that she would plead a headache as her excuse for not going to the Festival, and would say that she was going to bed. Then, when everyone was gone, she would take one of the bicycles from the rack in the garage and ride to Mr. Berthon's house. Maybe he would step outside for a breath of fresh air and she could talk to him alone, without Lucienne. If he didn't do that, she would ring the doorbell and ask to speak to him alone. She could tell Lucienne that she needed Mr. Berthon's help in trying to make up all the studies she had missed during her month's absence from his classes.

The first part of Jane's plan worked perfectly. Her white face at the dinner table was proof enough of her headache. Miss Brand, herself, after looking at Jane's wan face, suggested that it might be best for her to stay at the school, instead of going with the others.

She was in bed, pretending to be half-asleep, when Ellin came up to the room for one last visit, to make sure that she was all right, before they departed for Hollytown.

"Guess who's going with us, Janie," she whispered. "Mr. Berthon! He just arrived and said that his sister had gone back to town, leaving him alone, so he had decided to go with us. He said that he might not stay long, but a minute of Paul Berthon is worth three hours of the other professors. Milly is so excited that she is fairly goggle-eyed. She rushed right over to her room and came back with her best hat, instead of the old felt she had been wearing. Even Cornelia has come down off her high horse and is acting almost human."

Jane tried to act disappointed, but, inside, she was quivering with excitement. Things were working out even better than she had dared to hope. Lucienne was out of the way. The little stone cottage would be empty, so she could look around without being seen. And Mr. Berthon would probably come home early, alone, and she would be able to have a talk with him and still be home in bed when Ellin returned.

She forced herself to lie quietly until she heard the sounds of the departing cars. Then she slid out of bed to dress quickly in a dark blue sweater and skirt. Finally, muffled in a long, dark coat, she slipped down the stairs and through the empty halls. Cautiously she opened the front doors and peered outside. She breathed a sigh of relief, when she saw that Mr. Gridley was not in sight, and scurried noiselessly across the lawn to the garage.

It was dark and deserted, as she had thought it would be, the new chauffeur having driven one of the cars to the Festival. The bicycles, which the girls used in recreation hours, were parked in a neat row in the long rack. It was the work of only a minute to pull one free and to pick up one of the flashlights, which were always kept on a bench inside the door. Then, with the flashlight tucked into her coat pocket, Jane pedaled swiftly away. Luck was with her and she reached the path, which followed the river, without even seeing Mr. Gridley.

Three quarters of an hour later Jane saw the gray blotch which was Paul Berthon's cottage. She slid from her bicycle about fifty yards from the house and hid it in a thick clump of bushes. Then, cautiously, she tiptoed forward toward the cottage. She didn't want any chance caller or any passerby on the road to see her.

Not a light shone from the windows of the cottage. It was a gray ghost house in the darkness.

Jane wondered why she wasn't afraid. But, somehow, her excitement seemed to have driven away all traces of fear.

Noiselessly she crossed the little garden toward the house, keeping close to the shadows of the shrubbery. Then, just as she reached the edge of an open space and hesitated before venturing forth from the deep shadows in which she stood, she saw a movement of the leaves of the bushes at the distant corner of the cottage.

She stood still, scarcely breathing, her eyes straining toward those wavering branches. Someone was there. Someone was moving stealthily toward the house from the opposite direction!

CHAPTER NINE

THE HIDDEN ROOM

As Jane Withers watched, holding her breath, a shadowy figure stepped from the shrubbery and darted around the corner of the cottage. A few seconds later she heard the faint sound of lightly scraping wood. A window was being opened.

Then there was only silence.

Afterward, when Jane thought about that moment, she wondered why she did not turn and run as rapidly as her legs and the bicycle would carry her. But she didn't. Instead, she waited in a dead silence, which made her pounding heart sound like a noisy alarm clock.

Then, finally, when there was no other sound from the cottage, she moved stealthily forward, running lightly across the soft grass of the open space to the protecting shadows of the walls of the house. Hugging those walls, she crept toward the corner around which that dark figure had vanished.

Cautiously she peered around the corner. She found herself looking at the small, one-storied ell which Mr. Berthon had said was the storage room. One of the two casement windows was open and, through a narrow crack in its heavy draperies, shone a faint, dim thread of light. In his haste, the intruder had evidently failed to close completely the heavy curtains which shrouded the window.

Suddenly, as Jane stared at that dim line of light, it went out and the window was only a black oblong on the gray of the stone wall. Then the black square wavered and Jane knew that the intruder, whoever he was, was climbing through the window.

Clutching her coat collar high around her face and pressing her hand against her throat to try to quiet the beating of her pulse, Jane crouched against the wall, waiting and watching and listening.

The dark figure slid from the low window and dropped to the ground with a soft thud. Then again she heard that faint creaking of wood, as the two halves of the casement window swung shut. The figure paused a moment, then darted silently away into the shrubbery from which it had come.

Still Jane waited, motionless. She could hear the faint rustling of dry leaves, as the intruder made his way through the bushes. Then, far in the distance, there was the vague sound of a starting automobile motor—after that, silence.

Finally Jane moved forward. Her rubber-soled tennis shoes made no noise on the soft grass. She reached the window through which the dark figure had entered the cottage. It was tightly closed. Cautiously she tugged with her fingertips at the frame between the two sections of the window, but she could not move it.

The Window Was Tightly Closed

Jane knew that there must be some way of opening the window. The man had done it without noise or fumbling. So, while her ears strained to hear any faint sound in the shadowy garden, she moved her hands around the window's frame and across the diamond panes. But she felt nothing, except smooth wood and cool glass.

The window was low. It would be easy to slide across the sill and into the house, if only she could find some way of opening it. She *must* see what was in that room, with its heavily shrouded windows. Her eager curiosity drowned all thought of fear. Something told her that, beyond that solidly closed window, she would find the answer to the questions which were whirling through her brain.

Then, unexpectedly, her exploring fingers touched a small knob under the wide sill. She turned it—it moved easily in her fingers. The two sections of the window separated and swung outward, with that faint creaking, which she had heard when the intruder entered and departed.

With trembling fingers Jane reached through the open window and parted the heavy cloth of the inner draperies. Beyond was only darkness. She listened. There was no sound. She did not dare to use her flashlight while she was standing outside. So, with a deep breath, she pulled herself up on the sill and slid across it into the room.

Again she stood silently, scarcely breathing, waiting, listening. But there was no sound or movement in the blackness. So, reaching behind her, she carefully closed the heavy draperies. Then she pulled the flashlight from her coat pocket and pressed the switch.

Slowly she moved the pencil of the flashlight's beams around the room. It was small and bare. The walls were paneled in dark wood and there were only two windows, both covered with thick draperies. A round table with a dark green felt cover stood in the center of the small room and, from the ceiling above it, was suspended a light with a circular metal shield. A mat-like rug covered the floor and there was one long, narrow bench against the wall.

A sudden wave of nausea swept over Jane. She turned off the flashlight and leaned against the table to support her shivering body. She knew now, after seeing the "hidden" room, that Mr. Berthon was guilty. He had lied, easily and quickly and cleverly, telling her and Miss Brand and Ellin that this was a storeroom, designed by the artist for his canvases and used by him for the storage of his books. And she remembered with a sickening clarity how he had rushed them away from the half-hidden ell and into the house for tea.

Jane could no longer have any doubts. Handsome, charming Mr. Berthon was a jewel thief! And there was no longer any doubt about what she must do. She must hurry back to Holly Hall and telephone Mrs. Dwyer. She must tell her about the finding of the velvet case and the discovery of this secret room, with its hidden knob, which opened the window, and its mysterious, dark visitor—

probably one of Mr. Berthon's accomplices. Then they would turn Holly Hall's distinguished professor of Romance Languages over to the police.

Numbly she groped her way through the blackness toward the open window.

"I've got to get out of here before I faint," she murmured to herself, fighting against the dizziness which made her head reel.

She reached forward to part the draperies and stood, frozen with sudden fear. Someone was moving through the shrubbery outside. She could hear the crackle of dead leaves. Whoever it was, moving so stealthily in the garden, must be coming to this room.

Panic-stricken, Jane backed away from the window. She circled the center table and huddled against the smooth wood of the wall.

Then she heard loud whispers, which echoed like thunder in the stillness of the little room.

"The window's open!" The words were uttered in a man's low, hoarse tones.

"Something musta happened to make Max leave in a hurry." That was another unmistakably masculine, but lighter whisper.

"You stay here. I'll take a quick look around outside, before we go in."

Jane pressed her body closer against the wall. Suddenly it moved away from her and she stumbled backward. One terrified hand clutched the corner of something big and

solid and clung there, stopping her fall. Soft cloth brushed her face and head. Jane's stifled cry of fright was
muffled by something heavy and woolly.

Jane never could understand why she didn't faint. But
she didn't. With one hand she tugged at the cloth which
smothered her and realized that she was touching empty
garments. The other hand still grasped the heavy object
which supported her tottering body.

Then, with a bright flash of memory, she realized
where she was. She was standing in the closet which
opened off the cottage living room, the closet storeroom,
which Mr. Berthon had shown to them that afternoon.
The smothering cloth was one of the coats, which she
had seen hanging there. The solidly heavy object under
her clutching fingers was a trunk.

The relief was so great that she sank in a limp heap
on the floor.

The sound of hoarse whispers roused her. She must
close that door into the hidden room, the door which had
so miraculously opened behind her. In the pitch blackness she reached forward, groping, and touched the edge
of the door. Her fingers felt the coldness of a narrow
metal strip and then, wonder of wonders, the door moved
noiselessly, sliding back into place!

Jane sighed with silent thankfulness. She knew that,
somehow, she had closed the door by the same good luck
which had enabled her to open it.

"I must have just happened to lean against the 'opener'

and that metal strip must be the 'closer'—the thing that closes it," she muttered hazily.

She crouched silently on the floor, listening. The panel of wood between the closet and the hidden, secret room was thin. She could hear the low murmurs of voices and knew that the men had entered the small, bare, concealed room.

The murmuring voices grew louder, as the men moved toward the center of the room. Above the pounding of her heart Jane could hear gruff words.

"Can't understand it. No sign of any trouble anywhere around."

"Max musta lost his mind, leaving that window open."

"The Chief'll have fits, if he hears about it."

The Chief! Was that Paul Berthon? Again Jane felt that sickening dizziness.

"Maybe it wasn't Max," one of the harsh whisperers said. "Max is never careless about anything. Maybe he hasn't been here yet."

In the pause Jane heard a faint sound of a metal click.

"He was here, all right. Here's his orders, in the regular place."

"What's he say?"

The other read what was clearly a message:

"I took the ice. I'll be back for the fire three tomorrow. Everything set. Boat sails midnight tomorrow."

Jane's head reeled. *Ice.* FIRE. What did they mean? Then, suddenly, she knew. Miss Ramsdell's diamonds.

They would be the "ice." Mrs. Dwyer's rubies. They would be the "fire." Oh, it was all so plain now! *Everything!* That secret room was the meeting place of the thieves, the hiding place of the stolen jewels.

She must get out of there. Escape from that closet. Telephone Mrs. Dwyer and the police. But how could she do it, with those men only a few feet away from her on the other side of that thin panel of wood?

Suddenly she remembered the door, leading from the closet into the cottage living room. If her luck were still with her, maybe that door would be unlocked and she could slip away through the house.

Cautiously she moved across the narrow floor of the closet and pulled herself up to her feet, her fingers gripping the frame of the door.

The moment she reached forward to grasp the door knob it began to turn! Slowly the door opened.

Before Jane could move, could try to hide among the clothes in the closet, a glow of yellow light from the living room flooded her and a dark shadow loomed before her in the doorway.

Terrified, she looked into the gleaming, narrowed eyes of Lucienne Berthon.

CHAPTER TEN

BOUND AND GAGGED

For a startled moment the girl and the woman stared speechlessly at each other. Jane Withers could find no words to speak.

The next instant Lucienne Berthon pulled a small revolver from the pocket of her coat and leveled it at the trembling Jane.

"What are you doing here?" she demanded roughly.

Her voice was sharp and harsh, not smooth and indolent as it had been, and there was no trace of a foreign accent in her words.

"I-I—" Jane began, too terrified to think.

"Move back," Lucienne ordered.

Numbly Jane stepped backward into the closet, staring at the little revolver which glinted metallically in the light from the living room.

Lucienne followed her into the closet. Swiftly she reached past her and touched the closet wall behind the shivering girl. Without turning her head, Jane knew that the panel door was sliding open.

"Turn around," Lucienne said.

Jane turned and looked into the secret room, lighted now by the bright, focused rays of the shaded light over the table.

Two men, with hats pulled low over their faces, moved forward in wordless surprise when they saw Jane, pushed forward into the room by Lucienne.

"Move!" Lucienne snapped and shoved Jane so roughly that her numb body lurched against the table.

Then Lucienne touched the paneled wall and the door slid back into place, closing Jane into the hidden room with the two strange men and Paul Berthon's sister.

"Who is *she?*" one of the men asked, looking at Jane.

"One of the pesky girls from the school," Lucienne answered briefly. "I found her in my clothes closet."

Even in her dizziness and fright, Jane was startled by the transformation in Lucienne. As she stood at the edge of the brilliant cone of light from the hanging lamp, she bore not the slightest resemblance to the graceful, lazy Lucienne of the week-end at the Dwyer home and of that very afternoon in the cottage. Now her thin body was tense. Her eyes were wide open and glittering. The slow smile was gone from her mouth, leaving her lips in a straight, hard line.

"How'd *she* get in *there?*" The man snapped the question like a whip lash.

Lucienne turned to Jane. "How did you get in the closet? Sit down and talk fast, my girl." She pushed Jane across the room and down on the bench.

Jane gulped. She must talk. But what should she say? She knew that she could not tell them the truth. If she did, she could hope for no mercy from those three, grim-

"What Are You Doing Here?" She Demanded

faced people, facing her. So she must not mention her suspicions or the finding of the velvet jewel case.

"Talk, I said," Lucienne ordered. "How did you get into that clothes closet?"

"I didn't feel well after dinner, so I didn't go with the other girls to the Fall Festival in the village," Jane faltered, her head aching with her frantic effort to think clearly and to say the right things. "I thought maybe some fresh air would help me, so I took one of the bicycles and rode in this direction. When I saw the cottage, I decided to stop for a minute and talk to Mr. Berthon—and Miss Berthon."

"What were you goin' to talk to them about?" one of the men interrupted.

Before Jane could think of an answer, Lucienne spoke. "All these silly schoolgirls have a crush on Paul, Mike," she said with a bitter laugh. "They look at him like a bunch of lovesick calves. Paul gets a big kick out of it."

Now Jane felt sick with shame. So Paul Berthon had been laughing at the admiration which she and Ellin and Bunny and Mary Lou and all the other girls had lavished upon him! What a bunch of silly fools they had been!

"So you came cat-footin' around to get a look at the handsome Paul, hey?" the man, named Mike, leered.

"Let the kid go on with her story," the other man grunted.

"Okay, Bart. Shoot, kid."

"I parked the bike and walked toward the house," Jane

went on with a gulp.

"Where'd you park it?" Bart asked quickly.

"Down the road a little way," Jane answered. Then she added quickly, "I thought that, if Mr. and Miss Berthon had guests, I'd go on without stopping. So I didn't come into the driveway."

"Okay. Then what?" Mike asked impatiently.

"There weren't any lights, anywhere. So I decided they weren't home. Then, just as I was walking across the garden, I saw a man slip over to that window." Jane nodded toward the window, which was now tightly closed and covered by its thick drapery. "I was so frightened that I couldn't move. So I stood where I was and he didn't see me. He climbed through the window. Then, in a minute or two, he climbed out again and went away. I was curious, so I walked over to the window."

"Was it open?" Bart asked.

"No. It was closed."

"How'd you get in then?" Mike barked.

"My fingers happened to touch that little knob under the sill. The windows swung open, so I climbed in. I had just stepped inside, when I heard your voices."

"And I suppose you just happened to touch the right panel in the wall an' the door opened into the closet," Bart sneered.

"Yes." Jane nodded. "That's exactly how it happened."

"What about closin' the door again, how'd you work that?" Mike wanted to know with a sneer in his voice, too.

"I just touched a metal strip on the edge of the door and it closed."

"It's a good story, kid, but it sounds mighty fishy to me," Mike said flatly. "People don't just *happen* to find knobs an' places on panels an' metal strips."

"You're sure nobody brought you in here?" Bart asked quickly, his eyes narrowed with suspicion.

"No. No one brought me here. I've told you the truth, honestly I have," Jane cried earnestly, pleadingly.

"I don't believe it," Bart said.

Lucienne spoke suddenly:

"She didn't come in through the cottage. I'm sure of that. All the doors and windows were locked and the closet door was locked on the outside."

"Someone could have brought her in, then shoved her in the closet an' locked the doors, when he heard us comin'," Bart said softly.

"I suppose you mean Paul!" Lucienne's eyes flashed as she faced him.

"That's *exactly* who I mean," Bart said, his voice still low, but with a menacing hardness in its tones.

"Well, you can get that right out of your head," Lucienne cried, her words shrill with anger. "Paul's on the up-and-up. You can bank your last dollar on him. Right now he's at that fool Festival in the village, fixing a good, strong alibi for himself, like he did last night with that silly old maid schoolteacher who's fallen for him like a ton of bricks. He's doing what the Chief ordered, staying away from here whenever any of you boys are due to arrive. He's too valuable, with all his connections, to get hooked up with any of you."

"Be careful what you say, Lucy. Don't forget the kid," Mike warned.

"She knows too much now," Lucienne shrugged her thin shoulders. "A little more won't help or hurt anything."

"I told the truth, Miss Berthon. Honestly, I did. Please believe me," Jane begged tearfully.

"It might be true at that, Lucy," Mike said thoughtfully. "Queerer things have happened."

"Well. I can't see's it matters much whether she's tellin' the truth or lyin'," Mike growled. "She's here an' she knows all about the place now. What gets me is, what're we goin' to do with her?"

"We'd better keep her until Paul comes and let him decide," Lucienne suggested.

"But you *can't* keep me here," Jane cried desperately. "They'll miss me at the school and look for me."

"They won't find you here. Don't worry none about that, kid," Bart grinned. Suddenly he stepped toward her and towered over her. "Did you tell anyone you were comin' here?"

"No. Not one person," Jane answered, looking up at him without flinching.

"She's probably telling the truth now, Bart," Lucienne

laughed maliciously. "All of those little Mamma's darl-ings have been using every possible excuse they could in-vent to have a few minutes alone with the handsome professor with the romantic eyes."

"When will Paul be back?" Mike asked shortly.

"He ought to be coming in any time now," Lucienne told him. "You can bet he won't stay a minute longer than necessary with those simpering schoolmarms and those silly youngsters."

At that moment the panel in the wall slid noiselessly back and Paul Berthon stepped into the little room.

"What do you mean by leaving the closet door open into the living room?" he said sharply to Lucienne.

Then he saw Jane Withers, huddled on the bench, and he stopped, surprised dismay on his scowling face.

"What is she doing here?" he cried in a low voice.

"One of your conquests has back-fired, my gay Lothario," Lucienne said and laughed shrilly and mirth-lessly. "This babe-in-arms came to see you, hoping for a secret rendezvous, and walked right into the little nest."

Something in her voice told Jane that she wasn't Paul Berthon's sister—that something was bitter jealousy.

"How'd she get in here?" Mr. Berthon asked quickly, ignoring Lucienne's outburst.

Briefly Bart told him what had happened, beginning with the finding of the open window by himself and Mike.

"What are we going to do with her?" Lucienne repeated irritably when Bart had finished the story. "We can't turn her loose now—she knows too much. And we've got to get her away from here, before the whole school comes tearing around on a wild hunt for her. You and your charming ways with the ladies got us into this, my friend Paul, and now you'll have to get us out."

"There's only one thing to do, Paul," Bart said quietly. "The little black boy won't never talk again."

Jane shuddered at the ominous meaning of his words. So poor old Henry had stumbled onto something, as she had, and now he was gone. And, from the looks of things, she was doomed to go the same way.

"Please, Mr. Berthon, please let me go," Jane sobbed, turning pleadingly toward the silent Paul. "If you do I'll promise not to say a word to anyone, ever."

"Don't be a fool!" Lucienne blazed at Jane. "If you've got any sense at all, you must realize we can't let you go now."

"Keep still, Lucienne."

Mr. Berthon's voice was knife-sharp. Then he turned toward Jane and smiled, looking, for a moment, like the Mr. Berthon of the classroom.

"Why did you come here, Jane? Tell me the truth."

For a moment Jane was almost tempted to blurt out the story of the finding of the jewel case and her determination to talk to him alone. But something in Mr. Berthon's grim eyes above his smiling mouth stopped her.

Suddenly she remembered that he was not Professor Berthon now. He was Paul Berthon, a jewel thief—the enemy of her friends.

"I told the truth, Mr. Berthon," she said dully. "Please believe me."

After all, it *was* the truth. She had come to the cottage hoping to see Paul Berthon, alone. But not for the impossible, romantic reason which the others believed.

"Help me, Mr. Berthon. Please help me," Jane begged eloquently, as he hesitated before speaking.

"Make up your mind what we're goin' to do with her, Paul," Bart snarled. "We can't stay here all night. We gotta get the kid outa here before they begin huntin' for her."

"Yes. Yes, I know," Paul replied, still hesitating.

Jane's hopes rose. Perhaps he would help her. He *couldn't* be as cruel and heartless as the others, she fervently prayed.

Then Mr. Berthon made his decision.

"Very well, boys," he said firmly. "We'll get her out of here now. We'll put her away in a safe place. Then we'll get word to the Chief and let him decide what's to be done with her."

"What's the matter, Paul?" Bart sneered. "Lettin' a pretty face weaken you? You didn't wait to let the Chief decide when you got rid of that darkie."

With those words, Jane's faint new hopes died and she sank in a limp little heap on the hard bench.

"This girl is much more important than the colored boy," Mr. Berthon said, with crisp authority in his voice. "I don't want to take the responsibility of deciding about her."

"Smart boy, Paul," Mike grinned admiringly. "This kid's disappearance is goin' to raise an awful howl. Even if you forced her to write a note, like you did the black boy, it wouldn't stop the whole country from lookin' for her. Let the Chief decide. We'll all keep our hands clean."

"That's the idea, Mike," Paul Berthon nodded.

Then he and the other three huddled together in the corner, talking in such low voices that Jane could not hear their words.

Finally, nodding in agreement, they turned back toward her.

"Please, Mr. Berthon. Please help me," Jane cried, holding out her hands toward him in one last frantic plea.

But Paul Berthon only looked at her coldly. Then he turned his back to her, opened the panel in the wall and disappeared.

Lucienne followed him, returning a few minutes later with a long coil of rope and a bandage, which she gave to the waiting Bart and Mike.

Jane watched them with listless, dazed eyes. She was too tired and numb to care much what they did with her now. At least, they weren't going to kill her, until someone, called the Chief, decided what they should do.

"If you don't fight us, we won't hurt you, kid," Mike

"Please, Mr. Berthon, Help Me!" She Pleaded

said, bending over her.

Jane lay still while they tied her wrists and ankles with the rope and blindfolded her eyes with the thick bandage. She knew that there was no use in struggling.

Strong arms lifted her and carried her. She knew that they went through the closet, because the hanging clothes brushed against her head.

A door opened and she felt the cool night air.

"Be careful, boys. Don't hurt her." That was Paul Berthon's voice.

They carried her a long distance over rough ground. Then a car door was opened and she was dumped onto the floor. Bart and Mike climbed into the front seat. She recognized their voices. The door slammed and the motor started.

The car leaped forward, bumping and jolting over the ground.

CHAPTER ELEVEN

OUT OF THE FRYING PAN

For hours, it seemed to Jane, the car traveled through the night. Sometimes, for brief minutes, it rolled smoothly and swiftly on level roads. But most of the time it lurched and jolted roughly over uneven ground.

Jane guessed that they were following unused side roads. She was too exhausted to be afraid. She even dozed for brief, blessed seconds of unconsciousness, until she was jerked back to wakefulness by the jolting of the car.

Finally the car stopped. The door opened. Strong arms pulled her out and carried her up some steps, across an uncarpeted floor, and dropped her on a hard cot. Someone threw a blanket over her.

She could hear the mutter of low voices. After a moment, she heard the crackling of burning logs and smelled the odor of a wood fire. The footsteps of two men thudded on the bare planks of the floor. The low voices went on and on. Jane, wide awake now, strained her ears to catch their words, but the murmurs were too indistinct.

Finally a door opened and heavy feet went down steps. Then a motor roared and the car drove away. A moment later one pair of feet returned. The door closed and the footsteps moved toward her.

Strong fingers untied the bandage and pulled it from her eyes. She looked up into the face of the man named Mike.

"Warm enough?" he asked.

Jane nodded

"Now, listen, kid, you'd better lie quiet an' take it easy. You're miles from nowhere, so screamin' won't do you no good. You could yell your lungs out an' nobody'd hear you. I'm not goin' to hurt you, so you might as well get some sleep. An' you don't need to try to figure on runnin' away. You're so far back in the woods you'd never find your way out an' we'd catch up with you before you got anywhere.—What's the matter? Ropes cuttin'?"

"Yes," Jane groaned, trying to shift her body into a more comfortable position.

The ropes which tied her wrists behind her back were cutting painfully into her flesh.

"Okay. If you promise to lie still, I'll loosen 'em."

"I'll promise."

Mike untied her wrists and tied them again, this time more loosely and in front of her. Then he loosened the ropes which bound her ankles.

Jane sighed with relief.

"Feel better?" Mike asked.

"Yes, thank you," Jane said.

Everything was so queer, like some fantastic dream. Mike, for instance. He was a member of a gang of thieves, but, in the flickering firelight, he looked like any ordinary man whom you might meet on the street. He still wore his hat and Jane saw that his dark suit was made of good material and that it fitted his thin, wiry body with tailored smoothness.

She glanced quickly around her prison and saw that it was a one-room log cabin, with only one door. That door was directly opposite the fireplace in which logs were blazing brightly.

"What are they going to do to me?" Jane asked quietly, when Mike moved away from her toward the fire.

Strangely enough, she wasn't as afraid of Mike now, alone in this cabin, as she had been in the secret room in Paul Berthon's cottage.

"I don't know," he answered briefly.

"Who's the Chief?" Jane asked suddenly.

The question seemed to startle Mike. He wheeled quickly and stared intently at Jane before answering.

"Don't know," he said flatly.

"You mean, you don't even know who he is?" Jane's voice was loud with surprise.

"That's what I mean. Nobody knows who he is. Now calm down, kid, and quit askin' questions. It's getting late, almost morning."

Jane snuggled down under the warmth of the blanket and pretended to close her eyes. But, through the veil of her eyelashes, she watched Mike.

He drew two chairs close to the fire and sat in one, putting his feet in the other. Then he pulled his hat lower over his face, leaned back comfortably, yawned with deep weariness and closed his eyes.

Jane lay quietly on her cot. She breathed evenly, pretending sleep. But she was wide awake, with a thousand thoughts racing through her mind. By this time, she knew, they must have discovered her absence at Holly Hall. She could picture the excitement of the search for her. She hoped that they would not telephone or wire her mother. They probably wouldn't, until they had had time to make a thorough search for her. So her mother would have one more night of peaceful sleep, before she knew that her daughter was gone—perhaps forever.

If they found the bicycle near the Berthon cottage—but they wouldn't. Paul Berthon and Lucienne were too smart for that. They'd find it first and hide it. And, when the searching party came to the house, they'd put on a wonderful act. Jane could imagine their anxiety and worry over her disappearance and their eagerness to help in the search. She wondered vaguely how Lucienne would explain her presence at the cottage, after Paul had said that she had gone back to New York. She'd probably think of some good story that would fool everyone. Or, perhaps, she had really gone back to New York, after Jane had been taken away, leaving Mr. Berthon to face the searchers alone.

Oh, how she hated herself for having fallen under the spell of Mr. Berthon's gracious charm! She shuddered when she imagined his laughter at her youthful "crush."

She could imagine now how he must have been sneering at her silently, when they had been talking that evening on the river bank. It was probably the unknown Max, or Mike, or Bart, who had been talking to him that evening and who had scuttled out of sight when she appeared.

It was all a bad dream, a horrible nightmare. It still didn't seem really possible that Paul Berthon was a thief, even after what she had seen and heard in that secret room in the cottage. Surely she must waken soon and find that she was dreaming.

But she was awake. She could see the little cabin and the sprawled man in front of the fire. Tomorrow an unknown person, the mysterious "Chief," would decide her fate.

Then, suddenly, with a startled panic, Jane realized her danger. All the numbness and dizziness left her and she saw clearly what lay before her. Her fate could be decided in only one way. They must close her lips, so that she could never tell what she knew. Their own freedom depended upon her silence. Mike could well afford to be kind to her tonight, knowing what awaited her tomorrow. Even a jewel thief must have some kind of heart and be able to feel pity for a doomed person.

She couldn't just lie there and wait for what was coming. She must do something. She must think and plan. She must find a way out of this terrible predicament.

A sudden, loud noise startled her so that she jumped

in nervous fright. Then she realized what it was: Mike was snoring.

Jane knew that the next few minutes offered her one chance of escape, now, while Mike was sleeping. He had said that there was no chance for her to escape through the woods. But she would rather die of starvation in the forest than face the "justice" meted out by the Chief and his gang.

Keeping a wary eye on the snoring Mike, she pulled her rope-tied hands from under the blanket and examined them. The rope was thin, but it was tough and the knots were firmly and expertly tied. There was no chance of wriggling her hands free and she knew that, the harder she tried, the more tightly she would pull those knots.

There was only one way to do it and that was to bite them loose with her teeth.

So she began the task, pulling at the knots with her strong, white teeth. Every time Mike moved, or even stirred, she slipped her hands back beneath the blanket and lay still, trembling.

At long last the first strand pulled free. Then the second. And, finally, the knot was untied. Jane's teeth ached and her jaws throbbed with the strain, but she felt like shouting with joy.

It was a comparatively simple matter to untie the ropes around her ankles.

The fire was a glowing mass of coals and a dull gray dawn was creeping through the unshaded windows, when she finally lay, free and unbound. Mike still slept in his chair, twitching and snoring restlessly, as if he were having bad dreams.

Jane knew that she must make no noise and no false moves. Gently she slid from the cot and stood on the floor. Mike did not stir. Cautiously she turned and spread the blanket back into place. If he should waken, he might, at first glance, fail to notice that she was gone.

She dropped to her hands and knees and began to crawl slowly across the room. She had decided that that way of moving was safer than walking. The width of the floor stretched endlessly before her. She forced herself to move slowly, carefully testing each wide board with her hands before she rested her weight upon it. She knew that a sudden creak would probably waken the sleeping Mike.

Once, when she was half way to the door, Mike stirred and muttered. Jane stopped, terror-stricken, crouching beside a rough table. In the tense silence her heart thumped so loudly that she was sure it would waken him. But, after a century-long moment of suspense, Mike settled again into the hollow of his chair and his snoring grew deep and rhythmic. Then Jane cautiously began her forward crawl.

She reached the door at last. Noiselessly she stood up and gently turned the knob.

The door was locked! And *the key was gone!*

With a sigh of despair, Jane realized that, in her wild

She Turned the Knob; the Door Was Locked!

hope of escape, she had failed to think of a locked door. She had still been blindfolded, when Mike returned to the room, after Bart's departure in the car. She had no idea where he had put the key. If it were in his pocket, as it probably was, she knew that there was no chance of getting it without waking him.

Tears of hopeless dismay filled her aching eyes. Only a door stood between her and freedom. But it might as well have been an ocean.

Her tear-dimmed eyes darted over the room, looking for some other possible way of escape. There were two narrow windows in the cabin and, dropping down to her hands and knees, Jane crawled toward the nearest one. But a brief examination showed her the futility of that hope. The tightly wedged frame was so crusted with dust and dirt and spider webs that she knew it had not been opened for months, perhaps for years. It would take herculean strength to force it open and, even if she could do it, the noise would arouse Mike.

Without much hope left, she crawled to the other window. Its condition was the same as the first.

As she turned away from the window, a smoldering log in the fireplace blazed suddenly with one last bright flare before it died into ashes. In the spurt of light Jane saw the glint of metal high on the frame of the door.

Her heart sang with new hope. Perhaps it was the key, hanging there, safely hidden from all eyes, except those of someone who happened to be standing by that one window.

Even in her new excitement, she did not forget her caution. Slowly she crawled back to the door and stood up. Standing on tiptoes, she reached upward until her finger tips touched the metal.

It was the key, a large, old-fashioned one, hanging on a rusty nail. In the dim gray light, which filled the cabin, she could faintly see its outline.

Straining every muscle of her legs and arms, Jane reached upward until she could grasp the end of the key. Then, with breathless care, she lifted it from the nail.

The key slid easily into the lock and the lock turned with only a slight grating sound. The door opened with only a faint creak. Jane slid through the narrowest possible opening and stood in the fresh air of the dark gray dawn, free at last.

Gently she closed the door behind her, so that the coolness of the early morning breeze would not waken the sleeping Mike. Then, buttoning her dark coat snugly around her throat, she darted away from the cabin and into the shadowy woods which surrounded it.

A rough, little-used road, scarcely more than a wide track, wound away from the cabin door. But Jane avoided this road, on which she might meet the returning Bart or even the unknown Chief, and plunged into the safe darkness of the woods. She had no idea where she was or in what direction she was going, but she didn't care. All that mattered was that, with each minute, she was putting more distance between herself and that cabin prison in which she had spent the night.

It was slow, tortured traveling, but Jane plodded onward, stumbling over stones and logs, crashing her way through dense underbrush.

Gradually the world grew brighter. The dark gray turned to rosy pearl. The trees and bushes, which had been dark, formless shapes, became blotches of flaming colors, scarlet, yellow, orange and still glossy green.

When the sun finally rose and its yellow light filtered down through the trees, Jane knew that she was competely lost in a pathless woods, but she also knew that the cabin, with her jailer, must be a long way behind her. She decided to move as steadily as possible toward the west, judging the direction by the sun.

"Then there's no chance of my traveling in circles and finding myself back at the cabin," she murmured. "If I keep going long enough in one direction, I'm sure to run into something, a house or a road or a person."

She remembered all the stories she had heard of people lost in the woods, who had died of hunger, thirst and exposure.

"But I'm strong and healthy," she reassured herself. "I could live for days without eating and I'll surely find a little water somewhere in these woods."

So she plunged onward, pausing only now and then to catch her breath and to still the rapid beating of her heart. Often she stopped, startled by some sound. But it was only the scurrying of a little animal or the swishing of a squirrel through the leaves.

The ground was sloping downward now and walking was easier. Jane was thankful for that, because, each time she stopped to rest, it was more difficult to force her aching, bruised body onward. Her canvas tennis shoes were torn and caked with dirt. The thickness of her coat protected her body, but her face was scratched by branches and her brown hair was hanging in a rough tangle.

"I'll have to find a place to lie down for a little while," she decided finally. "I can't go on much longer unless I rest."

Then she saw, through the trees, a faint glimmer of blue. Maybe it was a lake—and maybe there would be cottages where she could find help and rescuers.

This new hope gave her fresh strength and she staggered onward.

After a few moments she came out of the denseness of the woods into a sort of clearing and saw the lake, shimmering at the bottom of a gentle slope. It was a small lake, cupped among rolling, tree-covered hills.

And there, on the shore, half-hidden by a grove of trees, she saw the roof of what must be a cottage! A spiral of gray-blue smoke drifted upward above the trees so she knew that someone must be in the house.

Breathless with excited joy, she half walked, half ran, down the slope. As she drew nearer to the house among the trees, she saw that it was not just one cottage, but a group of several large, sprawling log cabins.

"It must be someone's hunting or fishing lodge," she thought vaguely. Perhaps only the caretaker would be there at this time of year, but he would surely have a car or a boat and he could take her to safety.

At last Jane stumbled onto the cleared ground which surrounded the cluster of log buildings. They were even larger than she had guessed, when she had seen them from the slope of the hill behind them.

Then she saw a man, sitting at a table on the veranda of the largest cabin. He was eating breakfast in the sunshine.

With a low cry, Jane staggered forward and managed to reach the steps. Then, for a moment, everything turned black and she knew that she was falling. But she didn't care. Gratefully she sank into the darkness. She had reached safety at last.

A voice pierced the black haze, a voice saying, "Here, drink this."

Obediently she opened her mouth and something hot and fiery flowed between her lips and down her throat.

Jane gulped, choked and opened her eyes, looking up into a sharp, blue gaze. The eyes belonged to a gray-haired man, who was bending over her.

"Feel better now?" he asked.

"Yes. Fine, thank you," Jane gasped the words and managed a faint, wan smile—in a minute she would be able to talk, to tell him what had happened.

A second man, this one wearing a starched white coat,

appeared beside the other.

"What's happened? Who is she?" the newcomer asked.

The gray-haired man laughed softly.

"The little bird that flew away has landed right back in the cage, I think," he said. "Lend a hand, Jeff, and we'll take her inside."

"Okay, Chief."

Then, for the first time in her life, Jane *really* fainted.

CHAPTER TWELVE

IN THE LION'S DEN

Slowly Jane opened her eyes and looked up at the rough log beams of a peaked ceiling. For a moment she didn't know where she was. Then, in a blinding flash, memory returned, bringing with it the black misery of despair.

All her painful efforts had been in vain. Instead of escaping, she had walked directly into the hands of the Chief himself! With a low sob, she remembered his words about the escaped bird coming back to the cage and, most vividly of all, she remembered the two words of the other man, *"Okay, Chief."*

Now there was no hope.

Weak and half sick with exhaustion, she looked dully around her. She was lying on a deep, soft couch in a small room with pine walls. The room was evidently a library because one wall was completely covered by filled book shelves. There was one wide window, but it was heavily shuttered, so the room was filled with a dim, cool light. There were several deep, comfortable-looking chairs and, next to the window, there was a broad desk.

Jane moved her aching body and realized that she was still wearing her coat and that her wrists and ankles were not tied. So the men who had put her on the couch and thrown a light, soft blanket over her knew that here there was no chance for her to escape.

As her brain grew clearer, Jane realized that the low hum she was hearing, was the murmur of voices. Then she saw that one of the two doors in the room was open a little way. Her new jailers, the Chief and the man whom he called Jeff, must be sitting only a few feet away from her, on the other side of that half-open door.

"How long you figure she'll sleep, Chief?" That was Jeff, of course.

"Hours probably." The Chief's voice was crisp and Jane thought of the sharp keenness of his blue eyes as he had looked down at her. "She was half dead, when she stumbled in here. She'd been wandering around the woods for hours. And that drink I gave her ought to put her out for a long time—I'd like to get my hands on that miserable Mike."

"He's scared as a rabbit after what I told him," Jeff chuckled. "He's a little soft, but he's a good man, Chief. After this, you won't have nothin' to worry about with him. He'll toe the mark right, scared to death he'll get dumped overboard. He was like a wild man when he came rushin' into my place to tell me the kid was gone."

"What did Berthon say when you phoned him?"

"I'd hate to repeat it—even to you, Chief." Jeff chuckled. "That guy's got a line of foreign an' American cuss words such as I never heard."

"That guy's got a lot at stake. If the kid ever got loose

Jane Heard the Murmur of Voices in the Next Room

and talked, his goose would be cooked right." The Chief spoke soberly. "You and I and the rest of us, even Mike and Bart, might get away, but there'd be no hope for him and Lucy. I'll bet he was relieved when you phoned him we had the kid, safe and sound."

"Relieved!" Jeff laughed. "He was so relieved he couldn't even talk for a minute. An' when Berthon can't talk, with *his* gift of gab, it's somethin'."

"You don't think any of them have any idea where she is, do you?" There was sharp anxiety in the Chief's voice.

"No, sir. Not the foggiest. I told 'em I stumbled on her in the woods, when I was goin' up to the cabin. I said I had her on ice in a safe place an' was goin' to turn her over to you right away. You'd take care of her, I said, an' see that nothin' was ever heard from her. All of them were so glad to know that she wasn't loose some place they didn't ask questions."

"What did they say about the search?"

"The school notified the police late last night, like you heard over the radio. They've organized searchin' parties an' they're combin' the country. The papers will carry the story tonight. Then all Cain'll break loose. They think it's another kidnapin'."

"And the bicycle the kid rode?"

"Berthon found it in some bushes near the house. He hid it in the little room. He got it out of sight, just before the first crowd arrived from the school to tell him the news the kid was missin'. Now he's out with one of the searchin' parties. But he's goin' to stick around the cottage as much as possible, in case we want to reach him."

"Where's Lucy now?"

"She hotfooted it back for town last night, after Mike an' Bart left with the kid. Everythin's under control, Chief."

"Everything but the girl. You'll have to get rid of her tonight, Jeff. And you'll have to do it alone."

"I wish you'd let me do it now, Chief. I don't like the idea of havin' her here all day, right in this house. Too dangerous. Liable to be searchin' parties nosin' around here any time."

"That's exactly why she's got to stay hidden here today. It wouldn't be safe to move her until night. You might run into one of those searching parties in the woods. I'm depending on you, Jeff, to take care of it right, as soon as I leave tonight."

"You know you can count on me, Chief. I even got the ravine all picked out. When they find her, they'll never know but what she was grabbed by someone an' then dumped out in the woods. They'll prob'ly figure she fell when she was tryin' to find her way back to the school."

An icy chill shook Jane's body when she heard those words. So that was to be her fate! She was to be found at the bottom of some deep ravine and no one would ever know what really happened.

"Everything okay at Berthon's?" The Chief was speaking again and Jane tried to control the shuddering of her body so that she could listen.

"Yes, sir. The Dwyer stuff was all that was left an' it's packed an' ready. I'll get it this afternoon an' take it down to the yacht. Then I'll come back here an' take care of the kid."

"No, you'd better bring it here and I'll check it and take it to the boat, myself," the Chief decided. "I've given Jimson orders to sail at midnight tonight. I don't want any slips."

"There won't be none," Jeff promised. "I'll get the stuff an' be back here by five this afternoon. That'll give you plenty of time."

"Good. Better look at the kid again."

Jane closed her eyes quickly and forced herself to breathe as calmly and evenly as possible.

She could feel Jeff's presence in the room and heard the rustle of his starched coat as he bent over her. She didn't move until he left the room and spoke to the waiting Chief.

"She's still sleepin', Chief. I'll give her a good shot in her milk or soup tonight. Then she'll never know what hit her."

"Good idea, Jeff. Listen! A car's coming up the road!"

"It's a searchin' party, looking for the kid, I'll bet. Didn't think they'd get up this far so quick."

"Work fast, Jeff. The closet off the library's the best place. Then you get out of sight until we see who it is."

At the words "searching party" a faint spark of hope flared in Jane's heart. She lay in a pretended half-stupor while Jeff swiftly and efficiently tied her hands and feet and thrust a choking gag into her mouth. Maybe, if she pretended to be partly unconscious, he would not be so careful about hiding her and she could attract the attention of the searchers.

But Jeff did not do a half-way job of binding and gagging her. The tough ropes cut into her flesh and the gag choked her. Then Jeff lifted her and carried her through the second door in the room into a dark closet. He wedged her slender body between two piles of blankets, so that, no matter how she wriggled and squirmed, it was impossible to make a sound.

He closed the door, leaving her in blackness, and she heard his swift, heavy footsteps hurrying away. He must have left the library door open because, in a few minutes, Jane heard the clatter of the knocker on the door in the living room and the sound of voices.

Desperately she struggled and lurched this way and that, trying to free herself, trying to scream. But she only succeeded in cutting her wrists and ankles with the ropes and in choking herself until the tears ran down her feverish cheeks.

Only a few feet away were friends—and she could not reach them, could not make them hear her smothered cries for help.

She couldn't hear the words that were spoken, but

she knew from the tones of the voices that the Chief was offering help and sympathy. Once he raised his voice and called to Jeff to bring water and cold beer for the searchers. Evidently, Jane thought bitterly, there was no one in the searching party who might recognize Jeff, whoever he was.

Then, after a long time, the searchers were gone and the house was quiet again.

Jeff opened the closet door and carried her back to the couch. He untied the cruelly cutting ropes, removed the gags and gave her a drink of clear, cold water.

"Want to wash your face an' comb your hair?" he asked and his voice was almost kindly.

Numbly Jane nodded.

So Jeff helped her up from the couch and, grasping her arm lightly, led her from the library, across the living room and down a hall to a clean, bright bathroom, sparkling with tile and porcelain. There he left her, but Jane could hear his footsteps in the hall outside the closed door, so she knew that he was standing guard.

As she bathed her face and hands and dried them on the soft towels, which were hanging on the racks, she examined the small room, surprised at finding such modern and luxurious fittings in a cabin far away from civilization. Jeff had hurried her through the living room, but she had seen its handsome furnishings and thick rugs. The Chief must be a very wealthy man, she thought vaguely, to own a place like this.

After one look at the narrow, frosted glass panes of the one window in the bathroom, Jane gave up all hope of making any attempt to escape from there. Besides, even if she did manage to climb through that window, Jeff and the Chief would catch her before she had gone a hundred yards.

So, after awhile, she opened the door and stepped into the hall. Jeff was waiting for her and, clasping her arm again, he led her quickly back to the library and the couch.

Worn out and dazed, she lay quietly, while Jeff covered her with the blanket and left the room.

Then the Chief stood beside her, looking down at her. She noticed with a hazy wonder that he was a fine-looking man, with smooth gray hair and an almost handsome face. He was dressed in dark lounging clothes that smelled of wood smoke and tobacco.

"Try to sleep again," he said and his voice was not unkind any more than Jeff's had been. "I'm sorry we had to waken you so roughly a while ago and put you in the closet, but it was the only thing we could do under the circumstances."

Then he was gone, leaving the door into the living room half-open.

"You'd better be on your way, Jeff," she heard him say, his tones crisp and authoritative again. "And don't answer any questions. If Berthon or any of the others ask where the girl is, just say you don't know, that I have her."

"Yes, sir. An' about the kid, do you think you can take care of her alone, while I'm gone? I mean, if the searchers come back this way."

"Of course I can. Just leave the ropes and gag on that table."

"Yes, sir."

"And tell Berthon for me that he did a swell job. I'll give him a little bonus, when I come back. He deserves it. There'll be plenty for all of us, with this stuff I'm taking out."

"I'll also tell him he needn't worry 'bout the kid," Jeff added. "She'll never spill any beans after you get through with her, I'll say. He was plenty worried about her breakin' loose. I don't blame him."

"You can set his mind at rest on that score, Jeff."

"Plenty worried about the kid." The words rang in Jane's brain, as she gently rubbed her bruised wrists. Maybe he was worried about her, and not just because she might get free and tell the story to the police. Maybe he really liked her a little, just because she was a young girl and helpless. He had seemed to like her. Maybe he wasn't all bad. And maybe, at the last minute, he might relent and try to save her from the bottom of the ravine.

It was a sad, forlorn hope. But it was still a hope.

Then she remembered that he didn't even know where she was, that no one knew except the Chief and Jeff.

Her fingers touched the charm bracelet on her wrist

and a sudden, wild idea flamed in her tired brain. She remembered that, during that long-ago, happy week-end at the Dwyers' home, Mr. Berthon had noticed and admired that charm bracelet, especially the little typewriter charm, which was so perfect in its tiny golden details.

"It's a perfect little typewriter," he had said. "It's amazing how they can make such amazing miniatures."

Maybe, if he saw it again, he might remember that happy week-end and his heart might soften. Jeff was going to him now. If only, in some way, she could send that typewriter with Jeff, without his knowing that he was taking it. It was her last and only chance. Faint as that chance might be, it was worth trying.

Quickly she unfastened the little typewriter from the bracelet. Next she bent the tiny golden wire hook on the charm, so that it would catch in Jeff's coat.

Then she moaned loudly and moved restlessly on the couch.

"See what's the matter with the girl," the Chief ordered.

Jeff hurried into the room and bent over her. Through her half-closed eyes she saw that he was wearing a rough tweed coat, instead of the starched white one which he wore when he was masquerading as a houseman.

"What's wrong, kid?" he asked.

"I hurt all over. Ache," she groaned.

"Sure you do. You been through a lot, kid. Wait a minute. I'll get you somethin' warm to drink. Then you can go back to sleep again."

He left the room quickly and spoke a few words to the Chief.

A few minutes later he returned, carrying a cup of warm milk.

"Here. Drink this," he said.

He slipped one arm under her shoulders and lifted her so that she could drink.

It was Jane's opportunity. She lifted one arm, as if to help herself upright, and the fingers brushed the sleeve of Jeff's coat. When her arm fell limply to her side again, the little golden typewriter was caught in the rough woolen material on the back of Jeff's coat sleeve.

She took two or three sips of the warm milk. It tasted funny and she knew that there was probably some kind of a drug in it.

"I can't drink any more," she said, gently pushing the cup away from her lips. "I just want to sleep."

"Okay, kid. Go to sleep," Jeff said and lowered her to the couch.

She closed her eyes and pretended to doze. Jeff watched her for a minute, then slipped from the room.

Jane held her breath, waiting, listening, hoping that the Chief's keen blue eyes didn't discover the little typewriter. Evidently he didn't see it, because, after a brief, low conversation she heard the sound of the front door closing, then the roar of an automobile motor. So she knew that Jeff was gone.

Silently she prayed that the little typewriter would not fall from his coat. She didn't think that there was much chance that he would discover its presence himself because she had placed it as far back, and under, his sleeve as she could reach. All she hoped was that it was not too far out of sight for Paul Berthon's keen eyes to see it.

She was so excited by her one last, desperate hope that Paul Berthon would see and answer her small, golden plea for help, that she thought that she would never be able to sleep again. But she did, dozing through the long afternoon in fitful jerks, when sheer exhaustion overcame her will to stay awake.

Several times the Chief came into the room and looked at her. But she did not speak. She heard him, pacing the floor of the living room, and knew that he was keeping a watchful eye on the windows, waiting for the first sight or sound of approaching visitors.

Finally she must have slept deeply, because, when she awakened, she heard the sound of Jeff's voice. The little library was dark now and through the half-open door she could see a flickering light, which must be the fire in the living room. The afternoon was gone and the dusk of twilight had come.

"They're all there, Chief. Beauties, ain't they? I always did like rubies."

There was a sigh of admiration in Jeff's voice.

"It's a good haul, Jeff." The Chief's tones were filled with satisfaction. "It's a shame to spoil those stones. But when the boys down in Rio get through with them Mrs. Dwyer herself wouldn't recognize her rubies."

"Nope. Nobody wouldn't ever recognize them, not even the police," Jeff said and chuckled.

"What did Berthon have to say?" the Chief asked suddenly.

Jane stopped breathing to listen.

"Honest, Chief, that guy's got ice water for blood," Jeff said slowly. "He's the coldest proposition I ever ran up against. He was there, waitin' to turn the stuff over to me. He'd just come in from one searchin' party, he said, an' was goin' out on another one. All he was worried about was that the kid might get loose an' talk. Asked me over an' over again if I was sure you'd do a good, thorough job of it. Now even you an' I, Chief, hate to do what we gotta do, an' we never even saw the kid before. But not Berthon. He never even batted an eyelash when he talked about it. All he said was, 'Be sure that the Chief does a good job, Max.' "

"We need more men like him, Jeff," the Chief said quietly. "When they think so much of their own skins, they take care of ours, too, you know. I heard over the radio that the police now think that the colored boy is mixed up in the kidnaping of the girl."

Jeff laughed mirthlessly.

"If they only knew how little he was mixed up in anythin' right now, except a lot of cold water. Berthon planted that idea with the newspaper boys, Chief. He's got a brain, that guy. He sure took care of the old darkie slick an' quick. An' just because the poor ol' fellow happened to stumble on him an' Ken on the river path one night. It was so dark, the old boy couldn't have recognized Ken's face. But Berthon wasn't takin' no chances, even though Ken had on a beard when the darkie drove him from the station the day he was a magazine writer. Honest, Chief, I tell you that guy hasn't got no heart."

Jane's last hope died with Jeff's words. Its place was filled with a violent hatred for Paul Berthon. Good, honest old Henry—so he had gone the same way that she was doomed to go!

Suddenly, she realized the meaning of the words she had just heard. So those magazine writers had been thieves, after all, members of the Chief's gang. And Paul had planned the robbery of Miss Ramsdell's heirlooms, just as he had probably planned the stealing of the rubies. It was all so simple and clear now. Why hadn't she realized it and called Mrs. Dwyer and the police, as soon as she had found the velvet case, instead of still blindly trusting that brutal Paul Berthon and hoping that he would be able to explain everything?

"What are you going to do 'bout little Lucy?" Jeff asked next and now there was real mirth in his low, chuckling laughter. "She seems to have transferred her affections from the professor to the rich sportsman."

"I'm taking her to dinner before I sail. She'll go to the boat with me to say good-bye."

"Never dreaming that all the ice is hidden under the soft rugs she's walking on," Jeff laughed.

"No. And no one will ever dream it, if you do your job at this end, Jeff."

There was a hard, unspoken threat in the Chief's words.

"You can count on me, Chief. You know that," Jeff said hastily.

"I know I can, Jeff," the Chief replied slowly. "I know that, as long as that trunk is buried at the bottom of the river, you'll never forget that you're Jeff Browning, not Max Brown, as the others know you, and you'll always remember that you've never seen the Chief."

"You can rest easy on that score, Chief," Jeff said in a strained voice.

"Okay. Now help me with the bag. I'd better be starting for New York."

Jane, lying quietly with tense muscles and straining ears, thought that she understood everything now. They didn't care what she heard, because she would soon be where she couldn't repeat it. Jeff was Max, the contact man between the mysterious Chief and the members of his gang. It was Jeff, whom she had seen that night in the cottage garden, a dark figure slipping in and out of the hidden room. It was Jeff who had left the note of instructions, signed "Max."

The Chief knew something about Jeff, something concerning a buried trunk, which would keep Jeff loyal to him forever. And the Chief, himself, was someone be-

yond suspicion, someone of wealth and importance, someone who could come and go as he pleased and take the
stolen jewels safely out of the country on his own yacht.

It was all so terribly simple now, and so terribly tragic.
Stronger than her fear for her own life, was her hatred
of Paul Berthon, who had duped kind, dear Miss Abigail,
trusting Miss Brand, the Dwyers, Ellin, herself, everyone.
Even honest old Henry, who had stumbled unwittingly
to his own doom.

Suddenly Jane realized that the voices in the other room
had stopped and that a tense waiting silence filled the
cabin.

A moment later Jeff dashed into the room, stuffed the
gag into her mouth, tied her wrists and ankles with swift,
rough fingers, lifted her from the couch and dumped her
quickly in the closet between the sound-deadening piles
of blankets.

As he hastily closed the closet door, leaving her in
smothering blackness, she heard the thud of the heavy
knocker on the cabin's front door.

For a moment there was silence. Then the knocker
sounded again.

Quick footsteps crossed the living room. It was probably the Chief, Jane thought, because Jeff's shoes had rubber soles and, no doubt, he had hurried into hiding as he
had done when the searching party arrived that morning.

The knocker sounded a third time and Jane wondered
why she could hear it so plainly. Then she saw that the

Jeff Lifted Her From the Couch

closet door was open a little way. She could see a faint
narrow line of dim light, shining from the living room
into the dark library. It was only a very narrow crack of
an opening, but it offered one last hope to Jane. In his
rushing haste, Jeff had failed to close the closet door tightly. Now, if she could make some kind of noise, she might
be able to attract the attention of the new arrivals, whoever they were.

She lay still, listening eagerly.

The front door opened and she heard the Chief's mellow voice, saying, "Good evening."

Another voice answered, "Good evening, sir," and the
blood rang in Jane's ears.

It was the voice of Paul Berthon!

CHAPTER THIRTEEN

A WILD MASQUERADE

Jane lay rigid among the blankets, scarcely breathing. Paul Berthon was here, only a few feet away.

But, instead of hope and gladness, she felt only an icy fear. The Paul Berthon whom she knew now was even more cruel and heartless than the Chief and Jeff.

"I beg your pardon, sir," Mr. Berthon was saying in the voice she remembered so well. "My car ran out of gas down the road a little way. I saw your lights and wondered if you could let me have enough to take me to the nearest filling station. My name is Berthon, Paul Berthon."

"Of course, Mr. Berthon," the Chief said heartily. "Come in. I'll get a flashlight and we'll go out to the garage and find some gas for you. My name's Gilbert, H. G. Gilbert."

Jane gulped chokingly. At last she had heard the Chief's name. She had heard that name somewhere before. Then she remembered. Lucienne had mentiond it that long-ago afternoon in the cottage, that afternoon which was really only yesterday. She had told the two investigators, Matthews and Drake, that she had had dinner with H. G. Gilbert, the well-known sportsman.

So "the Chief" was H. G. Gilbert! It was too fantastic

to be real. But it *was* real and Paul Berthon was talking to the Chief without knowing it. Only Jane and Jeff knew it, and Jeff was hiding somewhere, waiting for Paul Berthon to go.

"I've heard of you, Mr. Gilbert," Mr. Berthon said and he must have stepped into the living room because his voice was now loud and clear in Jane's ears. "I guess everyone has heard of your famous Whirligig and your other horses. I am sorry to intrude this way and bother you about the gasoline."

"You're not intruding or bothering me, Mr. Berthon. Glad to help you. I'm not doing anything, just waiting for my caretaker to come back from an errand in the village. Then I'm leaving for New York. Do you live around in this part of the country, or are you from New York, too?"

"I'm from Holly Hall. That's the girls' school near Hollytown. I'm a professor there."

"That's where the girl was kidnaped, isn't it? Terrible thing. I've been listening to the reports over the radio."

"That's what brings me up here," Paul explained easily. "I'm joining a searching party in Chippewa. We're going to comb the hills back of here tonight."

Jane's body burned with feverish rage at the glib lies of the two men. So Mr. Berthon hadn't seen her little golden typewriter after all. He was still pretending to be searching for her. Just chance had brought him to the home of his own Chief. That was certainly a grim joke on Paul. If only he knew to whom he was talking!

But maybe his story about the gasoline was another of his lies. Maybe he had seen the little typewriter on Jeff's sleeve and had trailed him here to make sure that she was successfully put out of the way. It was all so very confusing. Her head ached with throbbing pain.

"Chippewa's just a few miles down the main road," the Chief remarked.

"I know," Paul said. "Thought I'd have enough gas to get there. Didn't want to take the time to stop. They think they've found the trail of the missing colored man, the school chauffeur, in the woods back there."

"Do you think he had anything to do with the girl's kidnaping?" the Chief asked, anxious interest in his voice.

"I haven't any doubt about it," Mr. Berthon answered. "Of course, there's no proof as yet. But it all ties in together. And the police haven't been able to find a trace of him, since he disappeared."

"They ought to string him up, if they catch him," the Chief said almost viciously.

"They will." Paul's voice was grim and purposeful. "All I hope is that he's the right man, when they do get him."

Jane wanted to laugh, a bitter, mirthless laugh, as she listened to the two men, lying so smoothly for each other's benefit. What actors they were! The Chief had the advantage of Mr. Berthon. He knew who Paul was, of course. She could imagine the Chief's secret laughter as he played the part of an innocent bystander. She was glad that someone was fooling Paul Berthon, after all the people *he* had fooled.

"Well," Paul was saying. "I'd better not waste any more time. If you'll be kind enough to show me where the gasoline is—"

"Gladly," the Chief's voice was cordial. "Will you have a bracer before you start out? Probably have a long night ahead of you."

"Thanks. I'd like one. But I don't think I'd better take the time. They're probably waiting for me in Chippewa.— Nice place you have here, Mr. Gilbert."

"I like it. I spend as much time as I can up here. Always hate to leave. Ah, here's the flashlight. Now, if you'll just follow me, Mr. Berthon."

They were leaving and Jane knew sickeningly that, when Paul Berthon left that room, she would have lost her last contact with the outside world—the world of law and order. His voice had brought back all the happy memories of the school. It was the smooth, deep voice of the Paul Berthon whom she had liked and admired and trusted. Cruel and heartless as he was, maybe, if he saw her there, he would do something to save her from the ravine.

It was a bitter, hopeless thought, but anything was better than just lying there, bound and helpless, while he left without even knowing that she was anywhere near. It couldn't do her any more harm, to let him see her, even if it didn't do any good.

But what could she do to attract his attention, bound, gagged and wedged between heavy blankets? She lurched against the blankets. They moved a little. She twisted and turned, straining all the strength of her aching muscles. The piled blankets tilted toward the door. She took a deep breath and shoved her body forward with all her might.

The blankets toppled against the door with a dull, muffled thud.

Jane strained her vocal cords in a silent scream. All that emerged from her throat was a choked gurgle.

But the two men in the other room heard that soft thud and the gurgle.

"What was that?" Paul Berthon asked sharply.

"What?" the Chief asked, but Jane knew from the tenseness of his voice that he was only pretending surprise.

"That noise."

"I guess I didn't notice it. You get used to noises up here," the Chief explained calmly. "So many small animals and country sounds around here."

"But it sounded as if it were inside the house," Paul Berthon insisted.

Jane pushed her body forward again. The blankets toppled into the room, shoving the door open.

"There it is again," Paul Berthon cried. "Seemed to me it came from that room over there."

"I'll look," the Chief said. "But I'm sure it was outside. I heard it that time. Probably a woodchuck or something under the cabin."

The Chief moved to the doorway of the library and flashed his light toward the ceiling.

"Nothing here," he said quickly. "We'll take a look outside."

Suddenly a flood of bright light flashed over Jane. She blinked, half-blinded by the glare. But, before her eyes closed, she saw Paul Berthon, standing in the doorway behind the Chief, holding a flashlight in his hand.

When she opened her eyes again, the bright glare of the flashlight was gone and the Chief was turning on a shaded lamp near the door. In the soft glow of the lamplight the two men stood quietly, staring down at Jane, as she lay among the blankets behind the half-open door of the closet.

"All right, Berthon, now you know," the Chief said quietly.

"Yes, now I know," Mr. Berthon repeated slowly.

"Are you surprised?" the Chief asked with a grim smile.

"In a way, yes. In a way, no," Mr. Berthon answered and looked at the other man with honest admiration in his eyes. "I knew that the Chief must be a very smart and very powerful man. Since, automatically, power means riches in this world of ours, I knew that he also must be a very wealthy man. The fact that that man is the well-known and irreproachable H. G. Gilbert is a surprise, a very great one, I'll admit. But I was sure that the Chief must have been someone similar to a man like Gilbert."

"Very well said, Berthon," The Chief nodded. "Perhaps it is not such a mistake, your knowing who I am. Maybe this girl here unwittingly did us both a good turn in giving away her hiding place. Perhaps, with this knowledge, you may be of even greater value to me, and to yourself, too, than you have been."

"I hope so." Paul Berthon's voice was low.

Jane gurgled and choked. The gag had slipped and she was strangling.

But it was the Chief, not Paul Berthon, who bent quickly and pulled the gag from Jane's mouth.

"Here, give me a hand, Berthon. We'll put her back on the couch," he said.

The men lifted Jane onto the couch and the Chief loosened the ropes around her wrists and ankles.

Jane looked up at Paul Berthon, pleading in her tear-filled eyes.

"Please, Mr. Berthon, please help me," she begged through her swollen, parched lips.

Paul Berthon looked at her and she shivered at the cruel hardness in his eyes. Then, as he had done in the secret room at the cottage when she had begged him for help, he turned his back to her and walked from the room.

"Be quiet and we won't put the gag back in your mouth," the Chief ordered.

He strode from the room, following Mr. Berthon, and left the door open.

"Jeff!" the Chief called. "Come out. It's Berthon and he knows now."

Jane could hear the padding of Jeff's rubber soles when he walked into the living room.

"Max!" Mr. Berthon exclaimed in surprise.

"Yep, that's me, Paul," Jeff answered. "I'm Max to you an' Jeff to the Chief. What happened? I couldn't hear nothin' down there in the cellar. You'll have to bring me up-to-date. How'd Berthon get in on this?"

Briefly the Chief explained what had happened.

"I told you we oughta get rid of the kid this mornin'," Jeff reminded the Chief. "But you wouldn't listen to me."

"Not squeamish, are you, Mr. Gilbert?" Paul laughed.

"No, not squeamish, just reluctant." The Chief laughed too. "I know that such things have to be done, but I'll admit I like to be far away when they happen. You're not that way, I understand, Berthon. Jeff tells me you did a neat job with the colored boy."

"I'm not squeamish," Paul said briefly and there was a brutal hardness in his tones. "In fact, I'd always rather do the job myself, if possible. Then I know it's done right."

"If you're still worryin' about the kid, you can stop right now," Jeff said quickly "It'll be done right. You can bank on that."

"You can trust Jeff, Berthon." The Chief spoke with calm finality. "Now I'd better be going. It's getting late."

"Just a minute, Mr. Gilbert," Paul said quietly. "Before you go, I'd like to know just where I stand, now that the set-up is changed."

"Of course," the Chief agreed affably. "It's very simple. But the first thing to remember is that you must not call me 'Mr. Gilbert.' I'm still the Chief and the Chief only. And you still don't know *who* I am. Understand?"

"Yes."

"You all will go on as usual. Jeff will continue living in his little cottage in Chippewa, truck farming and acting as part-time caretaker of the Gilbert lodge. You will communicate with him, as you have done in the past. I will send my messages to him in our regular code, in the form of orders about the care of this place. You will continue to hunt up good prospects among the families of the girls at the school. And I'm hoping you'll be able to find a few more Dwyers. Lucy will work on the patrons of her beauty shop. Flossie, Ken, Bart and Mike will keep on with their jobs. Then, when I come back, the excitement over the kidnaping and the last jobs will have died down and we can decide what new prospects to start on. It's unfortunate for all of us that this girl had to blunder into the thing and cause all this extra trouble. We'll all have to lie low for awhile and I don't think any of you had better even try to communicate with each other, unless it's absolutely necessary. Is that clear?"

"Yes, everything's clear except one thing," Paul Berthon said quietly. "Where do *I* stand now?"

"You mean about the cuts?"

"Yes."

"Well, I guess that, since you are now in the inner circle, so to speak, and since you and Jeff are the only ones who know my identity, you should have the same cut. That's five percent more than the others. Is that okay?"

"Okay," Paul agreed. "I feel quite flattered to see that you aren't a bit worried about my knowing your real identity, Chief."

"Why should I worry?" the Chief asked lightly, with a ring of hard laughter in his voice. "A sentence for robbery would only mean the penitentiary, with a chance for parole. But a sentence for murder, even if it is an obscure colored chauffeur, would mean the death cell. Think that over, Berthon. Then you will understand why I'm not worrying. Ask Jeff. He knows."

"I see," Paul Berthon said coldly. Then he added in a milder voice, "And the stones? Are they safe?"

"Yes." The Chief's voice was matter-of-fact and business-like now. "Most of them are already on my yacht, safely hidden. The Dwyer stuff is in the false bottom of my traveling bag over there. I'm taking it to the yacht myself, and you can be sure that that bag won't leave my hands until it is safely aboard and hidden."

"Fine," Paul said pleasantly.

"Now you'd better get on to Chippewa and the search-ing party, Berthon." The Chief laughed heartily. "I'll trust you to think up a good story about your delay. Fate surely does funny things, doesn't it? You might have run out of gas anywhere, instead of right near this place. But I'm glad it happened this way. We're going to work well together, Berthon. I feel sure of that. Now I'll start for New York, soon as Jeff gets the gas from the tank in the garage for you. I'll give you a lift back to your car."

Somewhere near by, an automobile horn sounded twice.

"Somebody's comin'!" Jeff exclaimed.

"Another searching party, probably," the Chief said quickly. "Fix the kid, Jeff. Then get out of sight until we see who it is."

"Just a minute!" Paul Berthon cried in a loud, com-manding voice. "Stand where you are, both of you!"

Jane's heart almost stopped beating as she heard those sudden, unexpected words. In the silence she could hear the surprised gasps of the Chief and Jeff.

"Are you crazy, you fool?" the Chief hissed. "Put down that gun!"

"Don't move, I said!" Paul Berthon ordered. "I've got you both covered and, remember, gentlemen, I'm not squeamish. The game's over, Mr. Gilbert."

Then he raised his voice and called, "Come on in, boys!"

CHAPTER FOURTEEN

THE GLINT OF METAL

The door burst open and there was a rush of heavy feet.

Above the voices Jane could hear Paul Berthon's words, "Tie them up tight, boys. They're as slippery as eels."

Lying on her couch, almost too weak with surprise and joy to move, Jane sobbed softly. The miracle had happened. She was safe. She was free!

Then a dark figure was standing beside her. Gentle fingers were fumbling to untie the ropes around her wrists and ankles and a familiar voice was saying softly:

"Little Jane. Poor, Little Jane. But we've caught them, you and I. Whatever made you think to send me the little gold typewriter to tell me where you were?"

Jane didn't know whether to laugh or cry. Everything was so mixed up. The only thing that was clear was that the good old Paul Berthon was back again and that he had rescued her.

"Sending that typewriter as a token was a stroke of genius," Mr. Berthon was telling her. "The minute I saw it on Max's sleeve, I knew that he had been with you and that he could probably lead me to you. And I was fairly sure that, wherever you were, I would find the mysterious 'Chief.' So I followed him."

"Then your car didn't need gas at all?" Jane asked, bewildered.

"Of course not, my dear child," Paul told her and smiled. "I had to have some excuse to come barging in here. I followed Max and saw him turn in here. Then I went on into Chippewa and phoned my real Chief, a man who has a legal right to be so called. He said he'd send men right away. The two sharp blasts on the automobile horn were to be the signal, telling me that the boys were here and the place surrounded. You see, I didn't know what I'd run into here."

"But—but I don't understand," Jane faltered. "Who are you?"

"I'm a special investigator, Jane," he said gently. "I've been trying to track down this 'Chief' for months. I'll explain everything to you later. My one great regret is that you have had all this suffering, Janie. If only you hadn't gone to the cottage that night, everything would have been all right. But I had to go on through with it then. It was too late to stop. And it was you, really, who led me to the Chief. You do forgive me, don't you?"

"Of course," Jane sighed happily.

"Now do you think you have the strength left to go on for another hour or so until we finish the job?" he asked anxiously.

"Of course. But you'll tell my mother and Miss Abigail and everyone that I'm safe, won't you?"

"We can't tell them until the job's done, Jane. We don't

Gentle Fingers Untied the Ropes

dare. If the word got out that the 'Chief' of the gang had been captured and that you had been found, the others would scatter to the four winds and we might never find them. I know it's a hard thing to ask, after all you've been through, and after all the anxiety your family and the school have suffered. But, if you'll do it, it will mean everything in the capture of the entire ring. Can you do it, Janie?"

"Of course, I can!" Jane cried, sitting up and smiling. "I feel as good as new already. If I had a glass of milk and a sandwich, I'd be able to go on all night and finish the job."

"Good girl!" Mr. Berthon cried.

He led her into the next room. At first it seemed to Jane that it was filled with men. Then she realized that there were only four strangers and the "Chief" and Jeff, who sat, handcuffed together, on a couch between two men in dark suits.

Briefly and proudly Paul Berthon introduced Jane to the four newcomers. Then, at a low word from Mr. Berthon, one of the men hurried out of the room in search of food and milk for Jane.

Mr. Berthon settled Jane comfortably in a big arm-chair and turned to the telephone.

"You and I will start for the cottage in a few minutes," he said to Jane.

He picked up the receiver and put in a long-distance call for a New York number. There was a taut silence in the room as he waited for someone to answer on the other end of the line.

"Hello, Lucy," he said finally in a low voice. "Paul. I'm talking from a house near Chippewa. Just saw Max. He wants to see us tonight. Regular place."

Jane could hear the undertone of Lucienne's voice, far away in New York.

Then Paul spoke again. "You'll have to break the date. Leave a note for him with the elevator boy. Then get up here as fast as you can. I don't know what it's all about, but Max says it's important. 'Message from the Chief,' he said. Something's happened. Call Flossie and Ken. Bart's on his way down. He'll meet them at eleven o'clock, usual place. 'Bye."

He replaced the phone and scribbled hastily on a piece of paper. Then he carried phone and paper to Jeff and placed them in his lap.

"Call Bart," he ordered, "and say those words, exactly as I have written them."

As he spoke, he pulled a revolver from his coat pocket and held it so that it was pointed directly at Jeff's head.

With his free hand, Jeff lifted the phone and called a number.

"You still have a chance at a trial," Mr. Berthon warned in a low voice. But you won't have any chance at all if you make a slip now."

"Okay," Jeff muttered. "I know when I'm licked."

Then he spoke into the telephone:

"Hello, Mrs. Snyder. Can I speak to Bart, please? Max callin'." There was a moment's pause before he spoke again. "Bart, this is Max. Meet Flossie an' Ken regular place. Eleven o'clock. Somethin' important. They got the dope. Tell the missus you're goin' into town with me with a special load."

He paused, listening while Bart spoke, and when he talked again, his voice was louder and affable, evidently speaking for the benefit of the listening Mrs. Bart.

"Sure swell of you to help me out, Bart. Those folks gotta have the stuff early in the mornin'. Thought we'd go by the old Skinner road. Better drive out to the junction an' park your car there. I'll pick you up. An' bring along a bottle if you got one. It's a long cold drive. So long."

"Very well done, Max," Mr. Berthon smiled. "Now one more call. This time to Mike."

Again he wrote a message on a piece of paper and handed it to the scowling Jeff.

Once again Jeff called a number. This time Mike himself answered the phone.

"Meet me midnight regular place, Mike. Important," he said crisply; then he raised his voice and spoke with a hearty friendliness. "What you doin', Mike? Eatin' dinner? Well, say hello to the folks for me. Thought if you weren't doin' anythin' better tonight, you might like to have a little game. Better bring along your own dice. No, there's no use your drivin' 'way into town. I'll pick you up. So long, boy."

"Thank you, Max," Mr. Berthon said, taking the phone from Jeff's hand. "You should have been an actor. That was a perfect performance."

"Anybody'd give a perfect performance with a gun lookin' 'em in the face," Jeff growled.

The man returned from the kitchen, bringing a tray for Jane. Hungrily she ate the sandwiches and drank the cool milk. As she ate strength flowed back into her young body. She glowed with the feeling of safety and the thrill of the excitement of the last half hour.

She listened intently when Paul Berthon made another telephone call to a New York number. He gave brief orders to someone, telling him to surround the apartment house at a certain number on a certain street at exactly eleven o'clock. In Apartment 401 they would pick up three at once. Then men must be sent immediately to take over the H. G. Gilbert yacht. He paused a moment in his conversation and turned to the "Chief," who sat, silent and white-faced, beside the glowering Jeff.

"Where's the yacht moored?" he demanded.

The "Chief" told him.

"Where's the stuff hidden? You might as well tell me. The boys'll find it any way and they'll tear up the boat, doing it."

"There's a trap-door under the farther right hand corner of the carpet in the lounge," came the answer drearily.

Quickly Mr. Berthon repeated his words to the listener in New York. A moment later, his conversation completed, he turned toward Jane.

"As soon as you've finished your little meal, Jane, we'll be on our way," he said, smiling.

"I'm through now," Jane cried excitedly, setting down the tray with its empty plate and glass.

"Okay, boys, you two take your two prisoners in to town. And you two get into the railroad station at Hollytown. Keep out of sight until Lucy gets off the train. You can't miss her. She's tall and dark and she'll be wearing a dark suit, probably. She always does. She'll take the one taxi out to the cottage. Wait until the cab comes back, then come out to the cottage. It's a little stone house close to the road, three and a half miles north of Hollytown. I'll leave a light over the front door, so you can't miss it. That'll give me time to get Lucy and Mike in the hidden room. Jane will wait for you in the living room and show you the way into the room. Then we'll take both of them without a struggle."

"Like rats in a trap," the "Chief" mumbled.

"Exactly, Mr. Gilbert." Mr. Berthon turned toward him with a mirthless smile. Then he swerved back to the listening men. "If everything goes right, and I'm sure it will, we'll have the whole gang and all the stolen jewelry by one o'clock this morning."

"What about that bag?" one of the men asked, pointing toward the Chief's traveling bag.

"I'll take that with me," Mr. Berthon decided. "Then we'll bring it in with the woman and Mike. Jane and I will drive back to the cottage now and wait for our visitors."

A few minutes later the lodge on the shores of the little lake was dark and deserted. The three cars had rolled swiftly away into the night. One, with two grim-faced men and two sullen, handcuffed prisoners, had turned toward New York. Another, with two men in the front seat, headed for Hollytown. The third, with Jane and Mr. Berthon, was traveling rapidly toward the little stone cottage.

Jane spoke but seldom on the long drive. She was suddenly realizing how very tired she was and the cool night air made her sleepy. She felt so warm and comfortable, sitting snugly in the seat of the small coupe beside Mr. Berthon.

Mr. Berthon was silent, too. Most of the time, he stared straight ahead through the windshield. Jane could see the tense line of his jaw. But, when he turned to her, his face was smiling and his eyes were warm and kind.

"It will soon be over, Jane," he said once. "Then we can all get a good rest and I'll do my best to make you and Miss Abigail and your family forget the anxiety and suffering you've been through."

There were so many questions Jane wanted to ask him. But she was so weary. She dozed, leaning comfortably back against the seat.

Suddenly the car jerked as it slowed its rapid speed and Mr. Berthon's voice hissed in her ear, rousing her with startling suddenness.

"Look ahead, Jane. What's that in the road?"

"It looks like a car parked across the road," Jane whispered, peering ahead and sharing the tenseness of the man beside her.

"It's blocking the way," Mr. Berthon said. "That looks bad, Jane."

"Can we turn around?" Jane asked, shivering with new excitement.

"It's too late now. We're so close that they could easily get to us before we turned in this narrow road. Besides, it may be nothing except a minor accident of some kind and they've put the car in the road to stop someone for help."

The headlights of the coupe now shown brightly on the black sedan, which was standing across the road so that no other car could pass it.

"Listen, Jane," Mr. Berthon said quickly. "If there's any trouble, you jump and run. Don't wait for *anything*. Bring back help as soon as you can. The Chief's bag is locked in the luggage compartment and the Dwyer rubies are in a false bottom in the bag. Remember that. Get the bag later, if you can."

As he spoke he braked the coupe to a stop and reached into his coat pocket.

But before he could pull out the revolver which Jane

knew was there, a man's head appeared at each door of the little coupe. Jane saw the glint of metal in their hands.

"Get your hand out of your pocket quick, Berthon," a deep voice growled. "If you make a move, we'll shoot the kid."

Jane gasped. It was Mike's voice. She would have recognized it anywhere.

CHAPTER FIFTEEN

A MOMENT OF HYSTERIA

The man on the other side of the coupe spoke suddenly, close to Jane's ear.

"Get out of the car, Berthon," he said. "And remember, if you make one false move, I'll drill the kid."

That was Bart! Jane knew his voice instantly, too.

Mike opened the door on his side of the car and Paul Berthon stepped down to the road. With one hand Mike reached into his pocket and pulled out his gun, dropping it into his own pocket. Then he patted Mr. Berthon's clothes, searching for other weapons.

"He just had one gun, Bart," Mike said. "It's okay now."

"All right, kid, you hop out, too," Bart ordered and opened the door.

Obediently Jane stepped down into the road.

"Walk straight ahead an' get into the back seat of the sedan," Bart barked next. "We'll be right behind you."

Mutely Mr. Berthon and Jane obeyed. As soon as they were seated in the other car, Bart and Mike climbed into the front seat and, while Mike covered them with his gun, Bart wheeled the sedan and drove down the road a few yards. Then he turned off into a narrow side road and brought the car to a stop in the shadow of some tall bushes which lined the edge of a field.

"I'll get the coop," Mike said and hurried back down the road.

A few minutes later he drove Mr. Berthon's coupe into the side road and parked it behind the sedan. He turned off the lights and rejoined Bart on the front seat.

Bart had turned off the sedan's lights, so the four sat in darkness. The moon, which had been so bright a few nights before, was gone now and the little side road was shrouded in inky blackness.

Gradually Jane's eyes became accustomed to the darkness and she could see the white blobs which were the faces of Bart and Mike, looking at them over the top of the front seat. She felt a wild impulse to open the door and jump out into the dense blackness, but she knew that Bart and Mike had their hands on their revolver triggers and that she had no chance even to escape from the car, much less to run for safety and help through the unfamiliar country.

"You thought you were pretty smart, Berthon," Bart said in a low voice. "And you were. I grant you that. But Max was just a little smarter. He gave us a message right under your very nose."

How, *when* did he do it? Jane wondered. She tried to remember every word of the conversation in the lodge living room. The only time Jeff had had a chance to send any message was when he talked to Bart and Mike on the telephone. As she remembered those conversations, they had been perfectly harmless.

Mr. Berthon was silent and Jane could feel the tautness of his muscles under his coat as he sat close beside her in the darkness.

"We've never been entirely sure of you," Bart went on. "You were too new. The rest of us have been workin' at the game a long time. An' we all had something on each other. We didn't have nothin' on you. Even when you got rid of the darkie, you did it by yourself an' you were so slick about it that none of us had any proof of anything."

"So?" Mr. Berthon asked quietly.

"So Mike an' Max and I fixed up a little code of our own, to use just in case anything funny happened. We took Lucy in on it, too, but she thought we were crazy. She swore up an' down you were on the level with us. But then, we knew Lucy was crazy about you. That is, she was until she met up with this Harry Gilbert an' his millions. Well, the code worked tonight, all right."

"It certainly did," Mr. Berthon said dryly. "And, since it has worked so well, would you mind telling me what it was?"

"Go ahead an' tell him, Bart," Mike said. "We won't never need to use it again. I'd like the smart professor to know there are other smart people in the world, too. I'm stuck on that code."

"It was very simple, Berthon," Bart said. "When Max said to me that he had a 'special load' going into town, that meant you were headin' for town an' you had gone rat on us an' I was to nab you. He told me to bring a 'bottle' along. That meant a gun, because you were carryin' one. He said we'd go the old Skinner road an' meet at the junction. This is the old Skinner road we're on now an' the only junction it makes is with the road you were on, so he told me which way you were travelin'. Simple, ain't it?"

"Simple. And clever," Mr. Berthon admitted.

"My code was just as easy," Mike said. "A 'little game' meant the same thing as Bart's 'special load' meant, that you were headin' for town an' you'd given us the double-cross. When he said he'd pick me up, I knew he meant you were comin' along the road back there, because whenever Max an' I meet, we always meet here where the old Skinner road turns into the other road. Bringin' my own 'dice' meant my gun an' warned me that you were armed. Almost too simple, wasn't it, Berthon?"

"I guess it was. It completely fooled me." Mr. Berthon sighed resignedly.

"Now it's your turn to talk, Berthon," Bart snapped suddenly. "Who are you?"

"The professor of Romance Languages at Holly Hall," Mr. Berthon answered.

"Cut the comedy, Berthon," Mike threatened. "From now on, if you don't answer our questions an' tell the truth when you answer them, the kid there will get a rap over the head with this gun. An' it won't be any light little tap, either. So talk, my friend."

"*Now It's Your Turn to Talk, Berthon.*"

"Very well, Mike. You win. Ask the questions."

Again Mr. Berthon sighed.

"Who are you?" Bart repeated.

"I'm a special investigator, assigned to tracking down you and your gang and your mysterious Chief."

For a moment there was an amazed silence. Jane could hear the quickly indrawn breaths of the two men in the front seat.

"Max sure was right," Mike said after a moment. "He claimed there was something phony about you, right from the start."

"Where is Max now?" Bart asked.

"On his way into New York with two detectives," Mr. Berthon answered simply.

"Where was he when he phoned us?"

"At the hunting lodge of H. G. Gilbert, near Chippewa."

"What was he doin' there?" There was genuine amazement in Mike's voice.

"It may interest you two gentlemen to know that H. G. Gilbert is your mysterious Chief," Paul Berthon said slowly.

There was another silence, broken finally by two low whistles of shocked amazement.

"Did you get him, too?" Bart asked, after a breathless pause.

"Yes. He's on his way, handcuffed to Max."

"H. G. Gilbert!" Mike exclaimed. "It's hard to believe."

"Where's Lucy now?" Bart snapped the question. "When Max phoned me, I tried to call her at her apartment, but she didn't answer."

"I don't know where she is now," Mr. Berthon replied.

In the darkness Jane could see the shadowy motion of an upraised arm—and something gleamed palely at the end of that arm.

"Remember what I told you, Berthon," Mike snarled. "The kid gets it an' gets it hard, if you don't answer. Where's Lucy now?"

"She's on her way to the cottage," Mr. Berthon answered in a low voice.

"An' Flossie an' Ken?"

"I don't know where they are and that's the truth," Mr. Berthon said, moving to shield Jane from any possible blow. "They were supposed to meet Bart at eleven o'clock."

"I phoned them, too, soon as I could get away from the house after I got Max's call, but they didn't answer," Bart said quickly. "Maybe we still have time to head them an' Lucy away, before the cops get them." He turned a small flashlight on his wrist watch. "It's just ten-thirty. If we go fast, we can make the cottage by eleven. Then we can call the apartment an' maybe we can warn Flossie an' Ken in time for them to get away before the cops pounce. That's what they're goin' to do, isn't it, Berthon?"

"Yes."

"An' Lucy'll come in on the eleven o'clock train. That

will get her out to the cottage about eleven-twenty or twenty-five. We'll find some way to head her off before she gets inside an' the cops grab her. Where are your cops, Berthon? The ones who are waitin' for Lucy an' Mike?" Bart asked.

"They're at the Hollytown station, waiting for Lucy to arrive."

"They goin' to nab her there?"

"No. They want to get Mike, too."

"That works perfect, Bart," Mike cried jubilantly. "I was ordered to be at the cottage at twelve, so the cops are prob'ly plannin' to get there then. That'll give you an' Lucy an' me a swell chance for a good getaway."

"Okay, let's roll," Bart said, turning in his seat and pressing the starter.

"What about the professor's coop?" Mike asked, a jeer in his voice.

"Leave it where it is," Bart said decisively. "No one will discover it until some time tomorrow. An' by that time we'll be miles away an' the professor won't be caring what happens to his car."

An ominous undertone in his voice made cold shivers run up and down Jane's spine.

"Why don't we just finish the job here an' now?" Mike asked, as the car lurched forward, then swung around in the narrow road and headed back for the more traveled thoroughfare. "We know all we need to know. There's no use in botherin' with this extra baggage."

"No," Bart said firmly. "We might need him later to call off the cops, if our figurin' of the time goes wrong. Keep an eye on them, Mike."

So, while Bart drove at reckless speed, Mike knelt in the seat, facing the two prisoners, and his gun rested on the seat back, its muzzle pointing toward them.

It was a nightmare ride through the black night. Jane huddled close to Paul Berthon in silent misery and fright. He put one arm protectingly around her shoulders. On and on they rode, swerving and swaying with mad speed.

At last Bart swerved the car off the road and braked it to a sudden stop in a small grove of trees. Quickly the two men jumped from the car and ordered Mr. Berthon and Jane to get out.

"Follow Mike an' don't make no noise," Bart ordered. "Remember, I'm right behind you an' my finger's itchin' on the trigger."

So they marched in single file through heavy underbrush and over rough ground. Suddenly they stepped through a tangle of bushes onto soft grass and Jane saw that they were standing in the rear garden of the little stone cottage. All the windows were dark, as they had been that other night, which seemed so long ago, when Jane had stood alone in the shadows of that same garden.

"We'll go in the front door this time," Bart ordered. "Not through the window."

So the silent little procession filed around the cottage

to the front door.

"Open the door, Berthon," Bart commanded.

With firm, steady fingers Paul Berthon found his keys and opened the door.

"No lights, until we make sure the shades are drawn," Mike hissed.

While Bart examined the windows with his flashlight, carefully pulling together the heavy draperies, Mike covered the other two with his gun. When Bart was satisfied that everything was securely shielded, he turned on one small shaded light.

"Now the telephone," he barked. "We gotta warn Flossie an' Ken."

Silently Paul Berthon pointed to the instrument on a table.

Bart rushed to it and hastily called a New York number.

As he waited for an answer, the grandfather's clock in the corner boomed eleven. Quickly Mike glanced at his wrist watch.

"The clock's slow," he growled. "It's seven minutes after eleven."

Suddenly Bart's face hardened and he gently replaced the telephone in its cradle.

"Too late," he muttered. "A strange voice answered. The cops are there." Then he swung upon Paul Berthon and there was a livid, savage anger in his eyes. "You'll pay for this, my double-crossin' friend, and' pay for it tonight!" he cried in a low, strained voice.

Jane cringed but not a muscle moved in Paul Berthon's mask-like face. Jane knew that he was holding himself in that iron control for her sake. Alone, he would have put up a fight against the two. But he did not dare risk leaving her to their mercies.

Then Bart strode across the room and flung open the door of the clothes closet. He stepped inside and pressed the metal strip on the panel. The door into the secret room slid back and he walked in. He turned on the bright light above the table, then returned through the closet to the living room.

"Get in there," he ordered, nodding toward the hidden room.

Quietly Jane and Mr. Berthon moved through the closet and into the secret room. Bart and Mike followed them.

"This is where you're goin' to end your days, so take a good look at it," Bart leered.

Jane sank down on the bench, too weak to stand. But Paul Berthon stood erect, facing the two men, who lounged, guns in hands, near the open door.

"I'll make you boys a proposition," Paul Berthon said suddenly in a calm voice.

"We don't want to listen to nothin' you got to say," Bart sneered.

"Let him talk, Bart," Mike grinned. "It might be interesting. What you got under your hat, professor?"

"Just this." Mr. Berthon's voice was low and firm. "I don't care what you do with me. But if you'll let the girl go, and I guarantee that she'll give you a good two hours start before she goes back to the school—she's so worn out now that it would take her more than an hour to *walk* back to the school—I'll tell you where the rubies are and you can take them with you when you go. They'll keep you two and Lucy in luxury for the rest of your lives."

Bart and Mike leaned forward, sudden interest gleaming in their eyes.

"Aren't the rubies with the Chief?" Bart asked quickly.

"No. And they aren't here. But I know where they are," Paul Berthon stated flatly. "I'll tell you if you leave the girl alone. And there's no use trying to torture anything out of her, because she doesn't know where they are."

"But we can work on her until *you* talk," Bart said slyly. "We're not lettin' anyone go an' we're goin' to have those rubies."

As he spoke, he began to move slowly and threateningly toward Jane.

"What's going on here?" a voice spoke suddenly from the open doorway.

They all turned, startled.

Lucienne was standing there, looking at them with bewildered eyes.

"You got here at the right minute," Bart said with a

sneer.

"What are *you* doing here, Bart?" Lucienne asked. "I thought you were to meet Flossie and Ken. And where's Max? Paul said he was to meet me here." Then she stopped, staring at Jane. "What's that kid doing here? I thought she—"

"Listen, Lucy," Bart cried tautly. "I gotta talk fast." Quickly he told her what had happened.

"Why, you double-crossing cheat!" Lucy screamed hysterically and threw her handbag at Mr. Berthon's head.

He dodged and the bag landed with a loud thud at Jane's feet.

Numbly she bent and picked it up. It was heavy, heavier than any handbag could ever be. Suddenly Jane knew that there was a gun in it and that the one chance of saving Mr. Berthon and herself was in her trembling hands.

For a moment the others were paying no attention to her. Lucienne had leaped toward Paul Berthon, screaming with fury, her hands stretched toward him like sharp-nailed claws. Bart and Mike were trying to quiet her, to pull her away.

"Quiet, Lucy!" Bart was saying. "The cops'll be here in a minute. An' Berthon knows where the rubies are. We gotta find out. Listen to reason, Lucy."

In the wild confusion of that moment, Jane slipped across the room and through the closet, clutching the

Lucy Screamed and Threw Her Handbag at Mr. Berthon

handbag in her cold fingers.

Swiftly she closed and locked the closet door. Then she opened the bag and pulled out the gun, which she had felt sure was there. It was the same wicked-looking, small revolver which Lucienne had pointed at her that other night in the secret room.

As she held that little gun in her hands, Jane suddenly knew what she must do. Everything was clear. Without hesitation she rushed across the room, opened the front door and stepped out onto the stoop. Then she remembered that Paul Berthon had said that he would turn on the porch light to show the police the way. So she stopped long enough to press the switch. The she sped around the house to the window, which opened into the hidden room.

Gently she turned the knob and the window swung open. The faint creak was lost in the jumble of low voices in the room. Cautiously Jane parted the draperies a little way and peered into the room.

Bart and Mike were finally quieting the raving Lucienne. Paul stood silently, a streak of blood across his white face, where Lucienne's long fingernails had scratched a deep gash.

"Listen, Lucy, be sensible," Bart was begging. "Be quiet an' listen. We only got a minute or so to find out where the rubies are. We'll all be on Easy Street for life, if we get them."

Then Mike's startled voice cut across the low murmurs

of the other two.

"*The kid!*" he cried. "She's gone!"

As the three turned toward the door into the closet, Jane saw that the guns in Bart's and Mike's hands were hanging loosely.

"I'm here!" she shouted suddenly. "Drop those guns or I'll shoot. I've got Lucienne's gun and I've got my finger on the trigger."

Paul Berthon moved so rapidly that Jane scarcely saw his swift leap forward as he grabbed the nearest gun—Mike's—from his surprised fingers.

When the three swerved toward Jane's voice, their faces blank with shocked amazement, they faced Paul with Mike's gun in his hand.

"Drop that gun, Bart," he ordered.

Bart obeyed. The revolver clattered to the floor and Mr. Berthon quickly kicked it out of reach.

"Remember the gun in Mike's pocket," Jane called excitedly from the window.

"Good girl, Janie," Paul Berthon answered. "Keep them covered."

Holding his revolver in one hand, Mr. Berthon reached forward and pulled his own gun from Mike's pocket. He dropped it into his own pocket, then quickly searched Mike for other weapons. He found nothing, so he turned toward Bart and rapidly felt his pockets. But he had no other gun.

Mr. Berthon backed away from them. Keeping a

watchful eye on them, he stooped and picked up Bart's gun from the floor.

"Isn't it strange how quickly the tables can turn?" he asked quietly, a faint smile on his lips. "If you hadn't been so anxious to scratch out my eyes, Lucy, you three might still have the upper hand. Maybe some day you'll learn to control that temper of yours."

He moved slowly to the window and, still covering the three speechless criminals in the secret room, he swung his legs across the sill and dropped to the ground beside Jane.

"Run around to the front, Janie, and watch for the boys," he said gently. "I'll stay here and hold the fort while you're gone."

"Here's Lucienne's gun," Jane whispered and gave it to him.

Then she rushed around the house to the driveway.

She watched anxiously for several minutes until finally she saw two headlights far down the road. A few moments later a car pulled silently up at the side of the road and two men stepped out. Jane rushed forward to meet them.

Quickly she led them around the side of the cottage to Paul.

"We have one more than we expected," Paul laughed, but his laughter was grim. "They're in there and they haven't any guns. Jane will show you boys how to get into the room. I'll stay here, so they can't escape this way."

So Jane led the two men into the living room and through the closet door into the secret room where the three white-faced prisoners were waiting.

CHAPTER SIXTEEN

THE SUMMING UP

The next hours were a dazed confusion to Jane Withers. There were voices and noise and lights. After she unlocked the closet door and ushered the two detectives into the hidden room, everything became a sort of blur. She vaguely remembered the almost silent departure of Lucienne, Bart and Mike, handcuffed together.

At last she was in a car, wrapped in blankets, with Paul Berthon sitting beside her, holding her hand and whispering comforting words.

The rest was all a haze. The return to the school. The many strangers. The happy cries and voices. Her mother's voice, talking to her on the long-distance telephone, telling her that she would soon be with her. The smiling, tear-streaked faces of Miss Abigail and Miss Brand and Ellin. The gentle hands and starched rustling of Miss Wheeler, the school nurse, as she bathed her and rubbed her aching body and tucked her into bed. Then sleep, —deep, wonderful sleep.

When she wakened the next morning, the room was flooded with sunshine and Ellin and Miss Brand were sitting by her bed.

"Good morning," they said gently. "How do you feel?"

"Fine, thank you," Jane smiled, then she winced as

she stretched her body. "Except for a few bruises and little aches."

Then Miss Wheeler bustled in with a thermometer and other gadgets on a tray.

"Normal as normal can be," Miss Wheeler announced, reading the thermometer after Jane had held it in her mouth under her tongue. "I'll go down and send you up a good breakfast." She turned to Miss Brand and sighed. "Youth is wonderful, isn't it? If I'd been through what that child has, I'd be abed for a month."

"Is she able to go downstairs?" Miss Brand asked.

"Yes." The nurse nodded. "After she's had her breakfast. But you'd better take it easy for a few days, Jane."

"Why, I feel elegant," Jane cried, sliding out of bed.

"I'll tell the others you'll be down after awhile," Miss Brand said, moving toward the door.

"What *others?*" Jane asked.

"Everybody," Ellin told her. "They're all waiting for you down in the library, Janie. You're famous, don't you know that?"

By the time Jane was dressed, the breakfast tray arrived, carried by a red-eyed waitress, who cried when she told Jane how happy she was that she was back home, safe and sound.

"The whole place has been almost crazy, until Mr. Berthon telephoned last night," Ellin said, when the waitress was gone.

She dried her eyes with a damp handkerchief, as she

spoke, but she smiled at Jane through her tears.

"I still don't quite understand everything," Jane said quietly. "It's all sort of vague to me. All I know is—"

"Eat, Janie. Don't talk," Ellin urged. "They're all waiting for you."

So Jane ate everything on the tray. It seemed years since she had had those sandwiches and that milk in the lodge.

Finally she was finished and the tray was empty. Arm in arm, she and Ellin walked down the stairs.

When they opened the library door, Jane blinked at the rows and rows of faces which greeted her with glad smiles. The library was the largest room at Holly Hall and it was filled to overflowing.

Miss Abigail was there, sitting in a high-backed chair and surrounded by all the members of the Holly Hall faculty. Mr. and Mrs. Dwyer were there, too, and beyond them were several strange men. Sitting around a table at one end of the long room were more strangers. All around the room, sitting in rows, were the girls of the school.

Everyone, even Miss Abigail, stood up, when Jane entered the room and Jane noticed with a shock of surprise that almost everyone was crying, even while they smiled.

Jane hesitated in the doorway, feeling suddenly shy.

The next moment Mr. Berthon was greeting her and leading her across the room to Miss Abigail.

"Good morning, my dear," Miss Abigail said and there

were tears shining in her eyes. "We are so happy to have you back with us and to know that you are safe."

The members of the faculty echoed Miss Abigail's words in a chorus.

Next Mr. Berthon led her to a gray-haired man with bright eyes and a smiling face.

"This is Mr. Grayson, Jane, the head of the investigation bureau. He wants to thank you for what you've done and to apologize for what you've suffered."

"Yes, indeed, Miss Jane." Mr. Grayson took her hand in both of his. "We owe you a great debt of gratitude. We didn't dream that this business would ever involve an innocent girl like you. Mr. Berthon and all of us are very, very sorry for what has happened and very, very proud of the part you played in it."

"I guess it's all my own fault," Jane faltered. "I sort of walked into it on my own hook."

She shook hands with the other men, when Berthon introduced them. He piloted her toward the strangers around the table.

"And these are the gentlemen of the press, Jane," he smiled.

The newspapermen and Jane bowed.

"What about pictures, Mr. Berthon?" one of them asked.

"You'll get all you want later, outside," Mr. Berthon promised and they nodded, satisfied.

Finally Mr. Berthon led her to a comfortable chair

"We Owe You a Debt of Gratitude," Mr. Grayson Said

and, when she was seated, everyone sat down. Then Mr.
Berthon turned to Mr. Grayson.

"Will you begin now, Mr. Grayson?" he asked.

"If I may make a suggestion, Mr. Grayson," Miss Abigail said quietly, and, when Mr. Grayson nodded, she
continued, "this is all so very confusing to most of us
that I should like to have you or Mr. Berthon begin from
the very beginning." She paused and spoke directly to
Jane. "I have asked all the members of the faculty and
all the girls to join us here today, Jane, my dear, so that
we may all greet you and hear the story of the terrible
happenings of the last few days. Once the story is completely told, I hope that all of us can try to forget it and
return to our normal lives."

"You are quite right, Miss Ramsdell," Mr. Grayson
said soberly. "I think Mr. Berthon can tell the story better than anyone."

"May I ask one question before Mr. Berthon begins his
story?" Miss Abigail asked.

"Of course."

"Exactly *who* is Mr. Berthon?"

Mr. Grayson smiled.

"Paul Berthon is the professor of Romance Languages
at Holly Hall and he is also a special investigator, de-
tailed to cover the activities of a gang of jewel thieves and
drug sellers, operating between this country and South
America," he explained. "Paul's particular assignment
was to discover, if possible, the identity of the leader of

the ring. This bureau knew the names of one or two of the members of the gang. But we did not want to take them into custody, until we had learned the identity of their so-called Chief. They, themselves, didn't know who their leader was, so it was impossible for us to learn anything from them. Therefore, Mr. Berthon was charged with the special duty of discovering the secret of this mysterious man, who directed the activities of the gang."

"I see," Miss Abigail said.

"I'll begin at the beginning, as Miss Ramsdell requested," Mr. Berthon said in his deep voice. "My mother was an American, my father a Frenchman. I was born in this country and spent my early boyhood here. Then my father's business took us to France and I was educated there and in England and on the continent. I was an engineer by profession but a serious accident forced me to give up the more strenuous phases of that work. While I was recuperating, I was offered a position as an instructor in languages at the Chenault School in Paris. I accepted and I liked the work so well that I stayed there for some time. From there I went to the Morrison School in London. So you see, Miss Ramsdell, my letters of recommendation were truthful, even though it was through Mr. Grayson's behind-the-scenes efforts that I was introduced to you and accepted here at Holly Hall."

Miss Abigail smiled and Mr. Berthon continued.

"It was in London that I first met Lucy Duval. She was teaching in a small and second-rate girls' school there, but, after knowing her for some time, I suspected that she had some activities other than teaching. From time to time Lucy hinted to me that we might work out a partnership which would be very beneficial to both of us. I told her that I would think it over and I began to watch Lucy and her friends closely. I soon began to suspect that they were involved in something illegal—dealing with drugs and stolen jewels.

"Lucy came to this country soon after I did and we renewed our friendship. I soon found that she was carrying on her same outlaw business here. I reported my suspicions to Mr. Grayson, who is an old friend of my family. He suggested that I continue my friendship with Lucy and, if possible, enter into her scheme. So it was done. I won't go into the long details of my winning Lucy's complete confidence and becoming a member of her gang of jewel thieves and drug importers. Then I heard about this mysterious leader, whom they called the Chief. And I discovered that Lucy and her co-workers had no more idea of his identity than I had.

"I met Max Brown, who was a sort of sub-leader of the gang, and we worked out the plan by which I was to pose as Lucy's brother and try to find a position in some exclusive school which catered to the daughters or sons of wealthy parents. Lucy was to buy an interest in some fashionable beauty shop with a moneyed clientele. In that way we could provide the gang with lists of possible victims and visit homes where we could learn details of house plans and family habits.

"I reported all this to Mr. Grayson and he insisted that I go through with this plan. We could have arrested Lucy and Max and the others whom I had met, but we knew that they were only tools of this mysterious Chief. It was the Chief himself whom Mr. Grayson wanted and it was my duty to find him at any and all costs.

"The plan worked beautifully. I managed to get this position at Holly Hall and Lucy bought her beauty shop, a half interest. The little stone cottage with its secret room was a perfect meeting place. The stolen jewels and the drugs could be hidden there while they were being moved. Max was the go-between, bringing us our orders from the unknown Chief. The Chief himself carried the stolen articles to South America and brought back the drugs.

"I had to prove my usefulness to the gang by arranging at least one 'haul,' as they call it, so I planned the theft of your diamonds, Miss Ramsdell, and for that I ask your forgiveness. I fully expected to be able to learn the identity of the Chief and to return the jewels to you before they were taken out of the country. Flossie Downing and Ken Burke, two members of the gang, did the actual work, after I gave them a plan of the school and the location of Miss Ramsdell's rooms and the jewels. Flossie and Ken posed as magazine writers, with forged credentials, and made a tour of the school to obtain information for an article on its architecture. You probably remember them. Flossie took your jewel case, while she was apparently examining the furnishings of your room, Miss Ramsdell.

"Then a peculiar thing happened. When Flossie returned to New York, she discovered that one of a pair of diamond earrings was missing. She was frantic about it and, of course, I did not dare to make any inquiries. Her only explanation was that, when she put the case in her handbag, the clasp came unfastened and the jewels spilled out into the bag. In taking her handkerchief or something from the bag, she may have pulled out the earring and dropped it somewhere without noticing it. But, since no one reported the finding of an earring and since nothing was said about it, all we could do was let it rest."

"Ellin and I found the earring and returned it to Miss Ramsdell," Jane cried. "We found it on the floor in our room, under one of my hat boxes. Probably that Flossie person dropped it in the station wagon and Henry set the hat box down on it and it got caught in the cord."

"Probably," Mr. Berthon smiled. "That is, no doubt, the answer to that mystery. So I am glad that you now have all your jewels, Miss Ramsdell. I was worried about that one missing earring."

He paused a moment, then went on with his story.

"Mrs. Dwyer's invitation put the best opportunity of all in my hands. I thought that, since it was such an important job, it would probably lead me to some contact with the Chief. When Lucy followed Mrs. Dwyer upstairs, she saw her return the paper, with the combination of the safe, to the envelope in the desk drawer."

"But Lucienne proved to those insurance company investigators that the sitting room door was closed and that it was impossible to see into the sitting room from the bedroom door," Jane interrupted excitedly. "And Ellin verified it, didn't you, Ellin?"

Ellin nodded.

"But Ellin forgot about the small mirror over the fireplace in the bedroom. The mirror was visible from the bedroom door and the sitting room desk was reflected in that mirror. Lucienne, standing in the bedroom door, could plainly see Mrs. Dwyer at the desk in the sitting room."

"Oh," Jane said with a sigh.

"Lucy also made a careful study of the house and grounds that week-end and learned a great deal about the habits of the family. It was Lucy, herself, who did the actual stealing of the rubies, with the help of a man named Bart Snyder. Since you and Mr. Dwyer were out that evening, Mrs. Dwyer, the front door was locked, but not bolted on the inside. Lucy and Bart arrived early that evening and hid in the shrubbery near the house. After midnight, when the watchman was making his round of the garages and the servants were in bed, they opened the front door with a passkey. Lucy entered the house and Bart returned to his hiding place in the shrubbery.

Jane Listened Excitedly to the Whole Story

"When you came home, Mrs. Dwyer, Lucy was hiding in one of the guest rooms. She waited until just before dawn, when she was sure that you were sound asleep. Then she slipped into your sitting room, through the bedroom door which you had said you never locked, found the combination in the desk, opened the safe, took the rubies, closed the safe, returned the paper to its hiding place. Bart gave her a signal, when the watchman was on the other side of the house, and Lucy climbed through your window onto that little balcony. Then, with Bart's help, she slid to the ground.

"So, when you wakened in the morning, everything was in its proper place. The front door was locked and bolted, as you had left it, and there was no sign of any forced entrance from the outside. That was how it was done."

Mr. Berthon paused again. In the silence everyone stirred, but no one spoke.

"I still do not understand how Jane happened to come to the cottage that night," Mr. Berthon went on, smiling toward Jane. "I think that she must have suspected something. When I found her bicycle, it was carefully hidden in a clump of bushes some distance from the house."

"I found the velvet ring case in the chair in your living room that afternoon, when we were having tea," Jane said in a clear voice. "I went to the cottage to talk to you about it. Somehow, I just couldn't believe that you were a thief, Mr. Berthon."

"Thank you, Jane," Mr. Berthon said quietly. "I always knew that Lucy's crazy love for jewels would lead her into trouble sometime. When the rubies were brought to the cottage, to be transferred to the Chief, Lucy insisted upon trying them on. She was wearing all of the rubies, when someone, I think it was a boy selling magazines, came to the front door. In her haste to get the jewels and the cases out of sight, she must have dropped one of the small ring boxes in the chair. If it hadn't been for that one misstep, Jane would never have been put through all the suffering she has known."

"And if it hadn't been for that one misstep, we might never have captured H. G. Gilbert," Mr. Grayson interrupted dryly.

"That's true," Mr. Berthon agreed, his face serious. "We didn't put the rubies back in the boxes, because we had to wrap them in small packages. So no one noticed the missing case. And never was I so startled in my life as I was when I walked into that little room and saw Jane. I didn't know what to do. If I had tried to save her, I would have given everything away. And, knowing that gang as I do, I knew that neither Jane nor I would ever have lived to tell the tale. I decided that the only thing to do was to let them take her to that cabin. I was sure that they would not harm her that night. They were scared to death of the Chief and would do nothing without his orders. So I planned to rescue her the next morning, some way. You can imagine how I felt, when Max phoned at daybreak and told me that she had escaped.

"Later in the morning Max told me that Jane was in the hands of the Chief. He claimed that he had no idea where she was, that he had found her and turned her over to the Chief. I was desperate. My one hope was that they would do as Max said they planned, and wait until night to do anything to Jane. I was sure that they would follow this plan, because it would have been too dangerous to have moved her during the day, with all the searching parties around. That gave me several hours to work and find a way to rescue her. I didn't dare call the police. I knew that, if I did, they would do something desperate to Jane immediately, especially since she now knew the identity of the Chief.

"That afternoon, when Max came for the rubies and I saw the little gold typewriter caught in the sleeve of his coat, I knew that Jane must have put it there. And I knew that she was wherever Max had been. So I followed him. And you all know the rest of the story. I told it to you last night. So I guess that's all I have to tell."

"Oh, no," Jane cried. "Where's Henry?"

"Just a minute," Mr. Berthon said.

He walked across the room and disappeared through the door into the hall.

A moment later he reappeared and Henry was with him, smiling and embarrassed.

Even Miss Abigail uttered a little cry of pleasure at the sight of the beaming Henry.

"Here he is, safe and well," Mr. Berthon announced. "You see, Henry happened to be driving home from the village one evening and he saw me, standing at the side of the road, talking to Ken Burke. We didn't hear the car, so there was no chance for Ken to disappear, as he did that night when you took a walk along the river bank path, Jane. Henry stopped the car to offer us a lift and, when Ken spoke, Henry recognized his voice. Ken had posed as one of the magazine writers, you know, and Henry had driven him to the station. Ken had rushed back from New York that same evening to tell me that one of the diamond earrings was missing.

"As soon as he heard Ken's voice, Henry immediately associated him with the theft of Miss Ramsdell's jewelry, so he waited for me on the school grounds to tell me his suspicions. That's what he was doing, when you saw us that night under the trees, Jane.

"Henry's smart. I thought that he might put two and two together and spoil my plans. So I told him the entire story and he agreed to disappear the next night. One of Mr. Grayson's men came after him and drove him to New York, after he had written that little note to Miss Ramsdell.

"I told Ken and Max and the others that I was sure Henry had recognized Ken and they were frantic. They said I'd have to do something to keep him from talking. So I agreed to take care of him. I let them think that Henry was lying at the bottom of the Hudson. Instead,

Henry's been living royally in a room over Mr. Grayson's garage, haven't you, Henry?"

"Yes, suh. But I'm suah glad to be back home. Providin', of coase, that I still got a job heah." He looked appealingly toward Miss Abigail. "Theah's that othah fella—"

"You'll always have a place here, Henry," Miss Abigail smiled. "The school can use two chauffeurs and you've needed an assistant for a long time."

"Thank you, Ma'am," Henry beamed and bowed himself out of the room.

Then Miss Ramsdell was standing. People were talking and moving toward the door. Jane was surrounded by newspapermen and finally she was on the front steps, being photographed alone with Mr. Berthon and Mr. Grayson.

At last everyone was gone and Jane was alone with Miss Brand and Ellin and Mr. Berthon.

"Will you forgive me, Jane, for letting all this happen to you?" Mr. Berthon asked pleadingly.

"Of course," Jane said quickly. "You're going to stay on at Holly Hall, aren't you, Mr. Berthon?"

"For the rest of the term," he said and smiled toward Miss Brand, who flushed rosily. "I have a contract, you know. But, when the term is over, I am enlisting in the engineering branch of the U. S. Army."

"Oh," Miss Brand gasped and the rosy flush faded.

"You'd want me to do that, I'm sure," he said gently.

Jane tugged at Ellin's sleeve and the two girls slipped away. Miss Brand and Mr. Berthon did not seem to notice their going.

"Well, all the excitement's over," Ellin sighed. "Now it's back to the old routine."

"Yes, but the old routine's a lot of fun, too," Jane said contentedly.

Arm in arm, the two girls walked up the steps of Holly Hall.

WHITMAN
AUTHORIZED EDITIONS

NEW STORIES OF ADVENTURE AND MYSTERY

Up-to-the-minute novels for boys and girls about **Favorite Characters,** all popular and well-known, including—

Ginger Rogers and the Riddle of the Scarlet Cloak
Deanna Durbin and the Adventure of Blue Valley
Deanna Durbin and the Feather of Flame
Ann Rutherford and the Key to Nightmare Hall
Blondie and Dagwood's Secret Service
Polly the Powers Model: The Puzzle of the Haunted
    Camera
Jane Withers and the Hidden Room
Bonita Granville and the Mystery of Star Island
Joyce and the Secret Squadron: A Captain Midnight
    Adventure
Nina and Skeezix (of "Gasoline Alley"): The Prob-
    lem of the Lost Ring
Red Ryder and the Mystery of the Whispering Walls
Red Ryder and the Secret of Wolf Canyon
Smilin' Jack and the Daredevil Girl Pilot
April Kane and the Dragon Lady: A "Terry and the
    Pirates" Adventure

WHITMAN
'GIRLS' FICTION

ADVENTURE—THRILLS—MYSTERY

Follow your **Favorite Characters** through page after page of **Thrilling Adventures.** Each book is a complete story.

WHITMAN
BOYS' FICTION

ADVENTURE—THRILLS—MYSTERY

Follow your **Favorite Characters** through page after page of **Thrilling Adventures.** Each book is a complete story.